"Will you marry me?"

Elise stared at Cole for a long moment. It wasn't the proposal she'd always imagined. No bended knee. No promised words of love.

She reminded herself that this was more of a business arrangement, and yet something inside her constricted.

Oh, come on, Elise! Here's a strong, good-looking man who has a home and a family, asking to marry you. And he's willing to offer it all to you! Just not love.

Cole grasped her hands in his much larger ones. Electricity skittered through her, making her feel as if every nerve was exposed. His eyes darkened, turned to a misty blue-gray. "Are you having doubts now?"

"No, no second thoughts," she said. "Yes, I'll marry you, Cole."

His features softened for a moment, and the baby inside her moved.

Elise felt as if she were hanging by her fingertips off a cliff. Was Cole the one pushing her over the edge? Or was he pulling her up to safety?

Dear Reader,

Not only is February the month for lovers, it is the second month for readers to enjoy exciting celebratory titles across all Silhouette series. Throughout 2000, Silhouette Books will be commemorating twenty years of publishing the best in contemporary category romance fiction. This month's Silhouette Romance lineup continues our winning tradition.

Carla Cassidy offers an emotional VIRGIN BRIDES title, in which a baby on the doorstep sparks a second chance for a couple who'd once been *Waiting for the Wedding*—their own!—and might be again.... Susan Meier's charming miniseries BREWSTER BABY BOOM continues with *Bringing Up Babies*, as black sheep brother Chas Brewster finds himself falling for the young nanny hired to tend his triplet half siblings.

A beautiful horse trainer's quest for her roots leads her to two men in Moyra Tarling's *The Family Diamond*. *Simon Says... Marry Me!* is the premiere of Myrna Mackenzie's THE WEDDING AUCTION. Don't miss a single story in this engaging three-book miniseries. A pregnant bride-for-hire dreams of making *The Double Heart Ranch* a real home, but first she must convince her husband in this heart-tugger by Leanna Wilson. And *If the Ring Fits...* some lucky woman gets to marry a prince! In this sparkling debut Romance from Melissa McClone, an accident-prone American heiress finds herself a royal bride-to-be!

In coming months, look for Diana Palmer, a Joan Hohl-Kasey Michaels duet and much more. It's an exciting year for Silhouette Books, and we invite you to join the celebration!

Happy Reading!

Mary-Theresa Hussey

Mary-Theresa Hussey
Senior Editor

Please address questions and book requests to:
Silhouette Reader Service
U.S.: 3010 Walden Ave., P.O. Box 1325, Buffalo, NY 14269
Canadian: P.O. Box 609, Fort Erie, Ont. L2A 5X3

THE DOUBLE HEART RANCH

Leanna Wilson

ROMANCE™
Published by Silhouette Books
America's Publisher of Contemporary Romance

To Melissa & Katy,
I love you both!

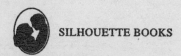

SILHOUETTE BOOKS

ISBN 0-373-19430-7

THE DOUBLE HEART RANCH

Copyright © 2000 by Leanna Ellis

This edition published by arrangement with Harlequin Books S.A.

® and TM are trademarks of Harlequin Books S.A., used under license.
Trademarks indicated with ® are registered in the United States Patent
and Trademark Office, the Canadian Trade Marks Office and in other
countries.

Visit us at www.romance.net

Printed in U.S.A.

Books by Leanna Wilson

Silhouette Romance

Strong, Silent Cowboy #1179
Christmas in July #1197
Lone Star Rancher #1231
His Tomboy Bride #1305
Are You My Daddy? #1331
Babies, Rattles and Cribs... Oh, My! #1378
The Double Heart Ranch #1430

LEANNA WILSON

believes nothing is better than dreaming up characters and stories and having readers enjoy them as much as she does. Leanna is the winner of the National Readers' Choice Award and Romance Writers of America's Golden Heart Award. Married to her real-life hero, she lives outside Dallas with their active toddler. While playing and reading to her son, she is cherishing the wonder of her baby daughter. But all the diapers and lullabies haven't kept her from writing. She's busy working on her next book, be it a Silhouette Romance, Harlequin Temptation or Harlequin American Romance novel. She enjoys hearing from her readers, so you can write to her c/o Leanna Wilson, P.O. Box 294277, Lewisville, TX 75029-4277.

IT'S OUR 20ᵗʰ ANNIVERSARY!
We'll be celebrating all year,
continuing with these fabulous titles,
on sale in February 2000.

Special Edition

 #1303 Man...Mercenary...Monarch
Joan Elliott Pickart

 #1304 Dr. Mom and the Millionaire
Christine Flynn

 #1305 Who's That Baby?
Diana Whitney

#1306 Cattleman's Courtship
Lois Faye Dyer

 #1307 The Marriage Basket
Sharon De Vita

 #1308 Falling for an Older Man
Trisha Alexander

Intimate Moments

 #985 The Wildes of Wyoming—Chance
Ruth Langan

 #986 Wild Ways
Naomi Horton

 #987 Mistaken Identity
Merline Lovelace

#988 Family on the Run
Margaret Watson

 #989 On Dangerous Ground
Maggie Price

#990 Catch Me If You Can
Nina Bruhns

Romance

 #1426 Waiting for the Wedding
Carla Cassidy

 #1427 Bringing Up Babies
Susan Meier

#1428 The Family Diamond
Moyra Tarling

 #1429 Simon Says...Marry Me!
Myrna Mackenzie

#1430 The Double Heart Ranch
Leanna Wilson

#1431 If the Ring Fits...
Melissa McClone

Desire

 #1273 A Bride for Jackson Powers
Dixie Browning

 #1274 Sheikh's Temptation
Alexandra Sellers

 #1275 The Daddy Salute
Maureen Child

#1276 Husband for Keeps
Kate Little

#1277 The Magnificent M.D.
Carol Grace

#1278 Jesse Hawk: Brave Father
Sheri WhiteFeather

Prologue

"And they lived happily ever after." Cole Dalton closed the book and ignored the tightening around his chest. "Happily ever afters" didn't happen so easily. Not at all in his life.

"Read another one, Daddy!"

"Not tonight, darlin'." He patted his daughter's leg which lay beneath the pale pink comforter. "You have school tomorrow."

"But I'm not sleepy." Haley stuck out her bottom lip.

"*I* am." He faked a yawn, stretching his arms out wide and opening his mouth until the sound of a creak came from his throat.

"What if I have a bad dream?"

"Then you can sleep with me." He gave her a light kiss on the top of her curly blond hair. Crossing the five year old's frilly room, he then turned off the lamp. Automatically the night light clicked on, glowing yellow in the corner, illuminating his daughter's upturned face. "Now be a good girl and go to sleep."

"Okay." Haley snuggled down into her covers and her hair splayed out across the pillow. "G'night, Daddy."

He could hear the chirp of crickets and croak of bull-frogs outside her window. He wondered why his ex-wife Paula had hated those sounds so much. To him, the comforting chatter seemed to embrace the ranch house. But it had never seemed serene when his wife had lived here, not with her complaining about the heat in the summer, the cold in the winter and the isolation year round.

Relieved that the nights were now peaceful and calming here on his ranch alone with his daughter, he whispered into the gray darkness, "G'night, sweetheart."

Before he could close the door all the way, he heard her soft voice ask, "Will they really?"

He paused, confused. "Will who what, darlin'?"

"Live happily ever after?"

In the dim light, Haley stared at him with those big, solemn brown eyes. His throat closed as if a fist had cut off his airway. Haley's constant barrage of questions always made him nervous. He never knew if he was answering the right way or about to scar his daughter for life. He knew firsthand that storybook endings didn't happen. But should he shatter that fairy tale for his daughter now? Or let her learn it the hard way, like everyone else?

"I guess so. That's what the book said." He leaned against the doorframe and felt a throbbing pain resonate in his chest. It was hard being a parent. More so, a single father. He didn't have anyone to consult with or confide in. But then he'd never had that with his ex-wife, either. "Now go to sleep, Haley."

"But, Daddy…"

He drew a shaky breath, not sure he wanted the answer to his next question. "What is it, baby?"

"How come we don't have a happy ever after?" Her

squeaky voice could have punctured a hole right through his heart.

His hand folded around the doorknob and squeezed until he could draw a full breath into his tight lungs. Slowly, he pushed the door open wider and reentered her room. The thick, pink carpet softened the clomping sound of his boot heels. His heart pulsed with self-doubts and recriminations. He carefully sat on the edge of his daughter's bed and tried to find the words to answer her woeful question. "Aren't you happy here with me, sweetheart?"

"Yes, but—" She stopped herself and shut her brown eyes.

He couldn't miss the quiver in her chin.

A cold clamp locked around his spine. Hadn't he tried to give her everything a little girl needed—cute clothes, nourishing food on the table, a happy home and all the attention a five year old could stand?

"But what?" he prodded, needing to know her answer even if he knew it might rip him to shreds.

"We don't have a mommy."

No they didn't. His ex-wife had lived as long as she could in the dust bowl of west Texas. She'd left, emotionally ripping out his heart and unbalancing their family. He'd tried to be both mother and father to Haley. Eventually, he'd admitted his deficiencies and hired a succession of nannies. None of them had stayed. They'd each found a lonesome cowboy, gotten hitched and moved on, leaving Haley and Cole once more on their own.

Maybe a little girl needed more than he could offer. Maybe Haley needed a mother more than she needed him. That drove a dull-edged blade through his heart.

His gaze shifted past the pink-curtained window to the darkness beyond. His great-great-grandfather had built the Double Heart Ranch with blood and sweat. But not alone.

His mail-order bride had stood by him through tornadoes and dust storms, droughts and epidemics. They'd built a life together and made their own "happily ever after."

Why couldn't he do the same? He'd tried love, but Paula had hated the ranch. Worse, she'd hated motherhood even more. Maybe he could advertise for a wife, find one without the usual dating frenzy and marry for convenience. This time, for a lifetime...for his daughter's sake. But could he trust a woman not to abandon them again?

Chapter One

"Having trouble with a Dear Jane letter?" Elise McConnell asked the studious cowboy sitting at one of her tables. She balanced a tray of food between one hand and her shoulder, and tried not to inhale the greasy odor of bacon.

The cowboy glanced up. His startling blue eyes narrowed into tiny slits of wariness that pierced right through her defenses. Deep crevices outlined his firm mouth, reminding her of the caverns in the nearby Palo Duro Canyon, hard and intriguing. He had dark brown hair that some barber had cut almost too short, leaving only a trace of a wave. He'd scattered several wadded up pieces of paper across the table and had scratched through his latest attempt with a stubby pencil.

Figuring he wasn't going to answer her, she placed his order of scrambled eggs, waffles and bacon in front of him and tried not to notice his wide shoulders and stern, uncompromising jaw. She'd made one mistake with a cowboy. She wouldn't make another.

Wishing she'd kept her big mouth shut, she asked, "More coffee?"

He nodded and pushed his mug toward the edge of the red-and-white-checked tablecloth. "Are you new here in Desert Springs?"

His deep rumbling voice made her abdomen tighten. Must be the pungent smell of grease, she assured herself. She hadn't had time to eat breakfast before she'd reported for work at a quarter to six and she was beginning to feel weak-kneed.

"Yes." She set the empty tray across a nearby table and reached for the carafe behind the cowboy's booth. Refilling his mug, she added, "I've been here almost a month. It's a nice town. Quiet."

She didn't tell him that she'd been dumped here, without transportation or money. It wasn't important. She was used to fending for herself. After leaving the orphanage at seventeen, she'd traveled from town to town, working odd jobs, attending a few college courses that interested her, but mostly looking for a place to call home. She'd thought she'd found a family with a cowboy. But she'd been wrong.

She'd actually started to like this little west Texas town and was considering taking up permanent residence. Besides, she didn't have any other place to go.

A hint of a smile curled the corner of the cowboy's mouth, denting his firm cheek with what she imagined must be a dimple if she ever witnessed a full-fledged smile. "It's quiet all right. The streets roll up at nine o'clock."

She gave a soft laugh. "That's okay with me. I'm usually soaking my feet by then anyway." Or asleep by nine these days. Being signaled by another patron of Chuck's Diner, she said, "Enjoy your breakfast. If you need anything else, let me know. I'm Elise."

Immediately she put the sexy cowboy and his worried frown out of her mind. She had enough troubles of her own. She'd do well to remember to keep her nose out of others' business.

Cole watched the talkative waitress walk toward another table and pour a cup of coffee for one of his neighbors. He couldn't help but notice the saucy swing in her step, the enticing sway of her apron ties along the narrow part of her lower back. A long auburn ponytail bounced between her shoulder blades. She wouldn't be here long, he figured. She'd grow bored with this one-horse town, especially when she realized there weren't many eligible men to flirt with and wrangle into the bonds of matrimony.

Turning his attention to his breakfast, he took a few bites of peppered scrambled eggs and then glanced back at the crossed-out words on the piece of paper beside his plate. He shook his head and fingered another wadded up sheet, one of many he'd attempted in his search to find the right words. Maybe this was a crazy notion. He hadn't told anyone about his plan. Would anyone understand? Hell, he wasn't sure he did. His friends would probably laugh until they turned blue.

Over the next hour, his gaze kept sliding away from the task at hand toward the new waitress. She had a quick, eager smile and bright discerning hazel eyes that were fringed with long, swooping lashes. Shaking his head at his own foolishness, he visited with several neighbors, folks he'd grown up with. They were ranchers and farmers, all about to head home to finish their chores, which was where he should go before picking up Haley from kindergarten. But he stayed on.

Four cups of coffee later, he shoved his fingers through his hair in frustration. He felt as jittery as a bull on the auction block. Maybe it was the caffeine. Or maybe it was that pretty waitress fluttering by his table and watching him so intently. This time, when she started to pour him another cup of coffee, he held up his hand. He'd had enough. Of the stout brew and his own stupidity.

"Are you a student?" she asked, propping a hand on her slim hip. "Trying to write an English paper or something?"

His frown deepened as he wadded up another page. "Working on an ad for the paper, but not having much luck."

"Yeah?" As quick as the weather could change in Texas, she slid into the opposite side of his booth. "It's slow, and you're my only customer left. Maybe I can help you out. I took an advertising class once when I lived in Dallas. What are you selling? Cattle, horses, an old truck?"

His throat dried up like Cactus Creek had last summer. The woman had soft expectant eyes that seemed to peer right into his soul. She looked as if she'd seen a lot in her young years and might not be shocked by the truth. Like others in this town. But his suddenly thick tongue stumbled over the words like a teenage boy talking to a pretty new girl at school.

"Is it a secret?" she asked, leaning forward.

In a way. But not for long. If anyone discovered his plan, gossip would spread like wildfire during a drought. That's what had him stumped. How would it affect Haley? He toyed with his coffee spoon, turning it over and over. Finally he found his voice and answered "Me."

Frowning, she dipped her chin. "Me what?"

"Me." He thumped his chest. "I'm for sale."

Her eyes widened. For a moment she only blinked. Then her jaw snapped shut. "Well, that's a new one." She pushed against the table to make her escape. "Pardon me for intruding."

He stopped her with a hand on her arm, stunning himself with a sudden need to unload his troubles. But why to this stranger? Maybe it was the sweetness of her smile, the knowing glimmer in her eyes or maybe it was the fact that she didn't know him. Whatever it was, he figured she might understand. And he desperately needed to bounce his crazy idea off someone. "That didn't come out right. It's not what you think. Let me explain."

She hesitated. Her eyes darkened, like oak leaves in late summer.

When he felt the muscles in her arm relax, he released his grip. His fingers burned where they'd touched her smooth bare skin. "Sorry."

She didn't answer, just stared at him with those perceptive eyes and waited. Waited for him to continue.

He shifted uncomfortably in his seat, settled his hand on his Stetson which lay on the seat beside him. He wished he'd kept silent. And kept his damn hands to himself. But he hadn't. Ever since Haley had broken his heart three weeks ago with her innocent questions, he hadn't been himself. He ran the palm of his hand down the top of his jeans-covered thigh. Now he owed this woman an explanation for his odd behavior.

What had the waitress said her name was? "Elise?"

She nodded.

"I'm Cole. Cole Dalton. I own a spread just on the outskirts of town." He wanted her to know he wasn't loco. He was local. He had roots here that went back four generations. She didn't have to fear him. But he saw only wariness and a thin slice of interest in her eyes.

She nodded again, still waiting for his explanation.

"Hell, maybe I *am* crazy." He thrust his fingers through

his already rumpled hair. "I'm really not trying to sell myself." But it felt like it.

He glanced around the inside of the diner. It was empty, except for the clattering in the back as Chuck, the owner, banged pots and pans in the kitchen, getting ready for the lunch crowd which would descend on the diner in about thirty minutes.

"You don't have to worry," she said, giving him a sympathetic smile. "I can keep things to myself."

He took a deep breath and then plunged in feet first. "I'm trying to find a mail-order bride."

Elise was sure she hadn't heard him right. Was this sexy cowboy with the dark-brown hair and sky-blue eyes trying to tell her he couldn't find a wife on his own? What kind of a town was this if a handsome man had to advertise for a wife?

Then she stopped herself. She'd fallen for a pair of friendly eyes and a dimpled smile before. Maybe this cowboy was simply feeding her a line, like Rusty had. Or maybe the women in town knew him better than she did...and there was a good reason why no one wanted to marry him. Still, the red hue brightening the tips of his ears told her he wasn't proud of the fact that he was taking out an ad for a wife.

Wary, yet even more curious by the minute, she asked, "Women that scarce around here?"

He shrugged. "Most are married, sixty-five and widowed, or young enough for me to risk a jail sentence."

"I see." But she didn't. It made about as much sense as her following Rusty to this desolate area of Texas where tumbleweeds outnumbered the cattle. She knew folks did odd things for strange, sometimes inexplicable, reasons. She admitted Cole had piqued her curiosity. She rested her elbows on the edge of the table and clasped her hands. "Amarillo's only an hour or so drive from here. You don't think you can find a wife the conventional way?"

"Tried that once. Failed."

Something in his voice hinted at deep-seated pain. Boy, could she relate. She hadn't fared so well in the love arena, either. She'd thought she'd been in love. Thought it had been mutual. But she realized now, she'd been looking for a home, a family, and she'd wanted—needed—more than that restless cowboy had to give.

"It happens," she said, recognizing the pain in her chest was not agony but embarrassment over her own foolhardiness. She had her own reasons for giving up on love, but that didn't mean she wasn't a romantic at heart or that she believed this good-looking rancher should. Surely he could find himself a woman who'd love him. "One failed marriage doesn't mean you can't find someone else."

"I'm not looking for love." His voice was deep and flat, almost devoid of emotion, and sent a scintillating shiver down her spine. "I simply want a wife."

"Why?" She cleared her throat. "I mean, excuse me, it's probably not my business, but couldn't you just hire a maid or something? For whatever it is you're looking for?"

Her face flamed. Maybe he wanted sex. And she'd just suggested he hire out... Oh, heavens!

His grip on the coffee mug turned his knuckles white. He had hard, calloused hands, accustomed to hard labor. She wondered if his heart was as battered as his hands. "I want a mother for my daughter."

His answer stunned her, knocking her back against the seat. Suddenly she saw this man in a whole new light. He was a single father, probably frustrated with his role, irritated with the stranglehold of family obligations. He probably wanted to dump the burden on some unsuspecting female. Rankled, she said, "Then hire a nanny."

"Been there already. I need someone more permanent than a hired hand who can up and leave at the drop of a hat."

Maybe he was thinking about his kid more than himself. Maybe. Then again, more than a wife he might need a whack on the head for a good attitude adjustment. "How old is your kid?"

His eyes brightened, the deep blue turning the color of a radiant summer sky, at the mention of his daughter. Then he smiled. Really smiled. Elise felt her heart lurch. She'd been right—he did have dimples. Which made her stomach flutter.

"Haley's five going on sixteen," he said.

As suddenly as her animosity had risen like a churning river, emotions dammed her throat. Her own father had never shown such pride in speaking about her. In fact, he'd never done anything for her but dump her at an orphanage when she was twelve days old and make darn sure she could never find him or her mother again.

But this man Cole...this rancher...smiled when he talked about his daughter.

She cleared her throat, trying to dull the dazzling effect of his smile. But she couldn't forget the shimmer of joy in his eyes or the vibration of pride in his voice when he spoke of his precocious child.

Remembering the way she'd given the nuns fits with her own antics, she gave a soft chuckle and fingered the apron around her waist. She could tell that Cole's daughter had wrapped her father around her little finger. It made Elise long for what she'd never had—would never have. "I was described the same way when I was a kid."

Cole's smile faded into a worried frown. He tapped his

fingers anxiously on the table. "She needs a mother. Not a nanny. Not a maid." He paused, and the sparkle in his eyes dimmed. "She needs more than I can give her."

The raw pain in his voice sounded like disappointment and made Elise's insides clench with understanding. She resisted the urge to reach out and touch this stranger, to reassure him, to soothe his troubled brow. This wasn't any of her business. Why did she always get too involved?

"Don't get me wrong," he said. "Haley's the best. She never gives me any trouble. But I know she's not happy." He ducked his head, as if ashamed of his confession.

Elise recognized despair when she saw it. She'd lived with it as a child. She'd learned to cope and face each day with a bright outlook, because she only had herself to rely on. To survive she had had to ignore the weak emotions of disappointment and overcome rejection and pain. If she hadn't thought something better was always around the corner, then she never would have survived puberty. "How do you know she's unhappy?"

"She told me." He gave a slight shrug, making his chambray shirt pull tight across his well-muscled chest. "Not in so many words. But well…she wants a 'happily ever after.'" He looked at her then, the blue of his eyes darkening with sorrow and regret. "You know, like in fairy tales. I didn't have the heart to tell her that doesn't happen in real life."

Elise understood Cole then—the hope he'd once had and the heartbreaking reality he'd experienced. Much like her own. She suspected he had a soft, compassionate heart beating beneath that rock-hard exterior. At least where his daughter was concerned. "So, you're going to give her as close a version as you can?"

"I'm going to try my damnedest."

The conviction in his voice made her believe him. Her

heart clenched into a tight knot as she met his determined gaze. His firm, square jaw told her he could do anything he set his mind to. For some crazy reason she wanted to help him. Uneasy with her attraction to the rugged rancher with the soulful eyes, she tapped her finger on his pad of paper. "Then you'll need a damn good ad. Maybe we should start with what paper you were thinking of advertising in? Desert Springs?"

"Not a smart move. I need a more populated place." He lowered his voice as if Chuck might overhear in the kitchen. "Where folks don't know me." He shook his head. "Not because I'm embarrassed or worried about what they might think. I simply want the marriage to look real. If folks here learn the truth, then it will only be a matter of time before Haley figures out it's all a charade."

An emotion Elise hadn't felt in far too long tightened her chest. This man would do anything for his daughter. His sweet tenderness touched her in a way no one had in years. "That seems wise. So maybe you should advertise in Dallas or Houston."

"Both, probably."

"Okay." She reached for his pad of paper and pen. "What kind of a wife are you looking for?"

His brow furrowed, pulling his dark eyebrows together. "Well...someone who likes kids. Obviously." He clasped his hands together, tapped his thumbs nervously. "Someone who's kind, sincere. Who'd be content to live on a ranch. A down-to-earth woman, who's not caught up in fashion or getting her nails done every week." His gaze locked on Elise's and made her swallow hard with anticipation. "A woman who wants to be a part of a family."

His answer struck a vulnerable nerve in Elise, and she felt the resonating pain all the way through her soul. Her heart pumped as if it might burst loose from the confines of her chest. He hadn't said "pretty, able to do backbreaking work and a good cook." He was offering a family. What she'd always wanted.

Trying to concentrate, paraphrasing his words, she scribbled notes on the page. The letters blurred as hot, aching tears pressed against the backs of her eyes. Ashamed of her weakness, she blinked them away as she had so often in her life and clenched the pen tightly.

Pushing back a glimmer of hope, she managed to ask, "Anything else?"

He nodded. "Someone who can make a commitment and stick with it."

She wondered if he were looking for the impossible. She'd learned long ago that promises were meant to be broken. At least by others. When she'd wrestled her turbulent emotions under control, she looked up at him and crossed her arms over her chest. "And what do *you* have to offer this make-believe marriage?"

This time he sat back against the seat. "What?"

"You want some woman to move out here and live with you as man and wife, tend to your child, and I assume do her wifely duties like cooking and cleaning and..." Heat stung her cheeks and she glanced away, unable to meet his intense gaze.

A palpable pause thrummed between them. Elise toyed with her pen, turning it over and over between her numb fingers. Why had she gotten involved with this man's problem? Why did he make her yearn for something she'd long ago given up on?

She didn't care if he found a wife or what he and this new wife would or would not do in an intimate setting. Good grief! What had gotten into her?

"Look," she said, breaking the silence, "you have to bring something to the table, something of value. Why would a woman who doesn't know or love you want to marry you? What are you offering?''

He ran his fingers through his hair, making dark brown tufts stand on end. The lines around his eyes and those bracketing his mouth deepened with tension. "I hadn't really thought in those terms." He rocked forward, then back. "But you're right. She ought to know what she's getting. I'm no lottery ticket. No real prize. At least that's what my ex-wife said."

She'd almost expected him to start cataloging his selling points. Rusty certainly would have. But she was beginning to realize that Cole Dalton wasn't like the showboat she'd followed out west.

After a slow, thoughtful breath, Cole stated, "I'm offering a home. A family." His mouth compressed into a firm, thin line. "I make a decent living. Nothing fancy. But I can provide for a wife and my child. I'm honest. Faithful. And loyal." He gave a sputtering laugh. "Jeez, I sound like a hound dog for sale."

She smiled at his analogy. He was anything but. And much, much more. Her pulse skittered at the thought of the possibilities. More anxious to hear his response to her next question than she cared to admit, she leaned forward, resting her chin on her hand. "Do you want more kids?"

He blew out a pent-up breath. "You ask tough questions. Are you sure you didn't take a class at the Barbara Walter's school of journalism?"

She chuckled. "I'm sure."

He turned his attention to the sun-splattered window that looked out onto the main thoroughfare that bisected Desert Springs. In the distance, a car horn blared. A furry dog pranced past, hunting for a scrap of food or his owner.

Elise watched Cole—the sternness of his profile, the decisive way his nose slanted toward his chin, the hard curve of his determined jaw.

Finally, his lips thinned, and he spoke. "I used to want a whole passel of kids. I was raised in the house where I live now. It's a rambling old place. Been on our land for four generations." He rubbed his palms together, and then clasped his hands, folding his long fingers, making Elise remember his gentle yet firm touch earlier. A warmth spread through her limbs, and she had a hard time concentrating on his next words. "I was an only child. It was a lonely existence."

It sounded heavenly to Elise. She imagined the total adoration of two parents being focused on one child—her. The air in her lungs compressed.

"My folks wanted more kids, but were never able to have any more. I always wanted to give them plenty of grandkids, to fill up all the bedrooms in the house. Hear the laughter..."

"The shrieks. The arguments," Elise added, remembering what it was like to grow up in an orphanage with at least twelve kids to a room. She'd always dreamed of a peaceful home, some place quiet and calm. She'd imagined a town much like Desert Springs where not much happened but where plenty of folks cared about each other, a place she could be a citizen, a neighbor, a member of the P.T.A. As she'd grown older, she'd started helping out with the younger kids. She'd enjoyed spending time with them, helping them get dressed, supervising their playtime. And she'd started dreaming of a family of her own.

She placed a hand over her stomach. Someday, she thought, someday soon. She wouldn't have all of her dream. But she'd have a small, precious part.

"Maybe that was simply a fairy tale I'd conjured up," Cole said. "Maybe it would have been more chaotic than

I imagined." He shrugged. "I guess I'll have to discuss the possibility of more kids with the woman who answers the ad to be my wife."

"You sound like there will be only one."

In an aw-shucks manner, he shrugged his broad shoulders. "I'll be lucky if there is one."

She had a feeling women would flock to this little town on the edge of nowhere to meet this tender cowboy and his child. Suddenly a part of her didn't want to help with the advertisement. Because she'd started contemplating something foolish and inconceivable.

Maybe, just maybe, his solution was the answer she'd been looking for.

One week later, Elise jounced the borrowed truck over the cattle guard and down the graveled drive toward a large, two-story farmhouse that looked better than Cole had described. And even better than she'd imagined. A white picket fence surrounded it. Tiny pink flowers in the yard battled the May heat. A solitary tree leaned toward the side of the house in the direction she'd learned the wind always blew here in west Texas. On either side of the house were sprawling fields dotted with rusty brown-and-white speckled cows.

A hot, stiff breeze blew through the open window of the truck and brought the scent of earth and animals. She parked in front of the house, breathed in the warm air, absorbed the sights and knew she'd finally come home. This was where she wanted to stay. Now, she simply had to convince Cole that she was the wife he needed.

The truck's door squeaked as she opened it and stepped out of the dusty cab. She fluffed out her loose-fitting skirt that felt sticky against the backs of her thighs from the oppressive heat in Chuck's non-air-conditioned pickup.

Sunshine warmed her shoulders and made her squint as she turned toward the house.

Maybe she should have called first. But then if she had, Cole might have turned her down flat. No, she had a better chance in person. Not that she had much to offer, she thought, in the looks department. She was of average height, but her features had always seemed plain to her. She was too pale and had too many freckles. She'd never measured up to other children at the orphanage who'd been adopted early. Meanwhile, she'd been left waiting... waiting for someone to want her.

Well, she wasn't going to wait any longer. She'd done her homework by asking questions about Cole Dalton. She'd learned he was a respected rancher in the community. No one had a bad word to say against him. All had confirmed what she'd suspected—he cared deeply for his daughter. What more could she ask for than an honest, upstanding man who loved being a father?

So what if love wasn't a bargaining chip? She'd realized a long time ago that Prince Charming wasn't going to ride up and save her. There wasn't always a perfect situation. She'd take what she could get. *If* she could get Cole.

She marched up the steps to the house and rang the doorbell. Impatiently she tapped her foot. Her nerves were tangled up like a ball of yarn. What would Cole say when he saw her? Would he laugh at her audacity? Would he turn her away? Her insides twisted and knotted, but she squared her shoulders. She'd been rejected before. If Cole laughed at her now, it wouldn't kill her.

"Hello." The voice came from behind her, and she swung around to find Cole at the bottom of the steps.

Her gaze stuck to his sweat-slicked bare chest. His rock-hard, suntanned muscles gleamed in the sunlight as if he were a marble statue. But she knew he was flesh and blood.

She'd felt his electric touch the week before. Now she couldn't stop staring at the play of muscles along his chest. Her mouth went bone dry, and she couldn't have swallowed to save her life.

Casually, he leaned against a white-painted post. With his thumb he tipped his cowboy hat backwards on his head, framing his face with shadows and sunlight. Slowly her gaze slid down the length of him. He wore tight-fitting faded jeans and a pair of scuffed boots. At that moment she began to doubt the wisdom of coming here.

"Elise?" he asked, his voice crisp as an early morning chill.

She nodded, feeling as if the heat had zapped her ability to think or speak. Her purse slipped off her shoulder, and she grabbed for it. Twisting the strap around her fingers and cutting off the circulation, she hoped blood would rush back to her brain and she'd be able to answer his simple question. "Hi."

His mouth remained firm and unmoving.

She scuffed the soles of her shoes against the porch planks. *What am I doing here?* The silence echoed between them. Cole lifted his Stetson, ran his fingers through his thick brown hair and then lowered the brim. It shaded his eyes and thoughts from her, unnerving her even more.

She had to get a firm grip on herself and take charge. "I came about the ad."

Cole's silence weighed heavily on her. He crossed his arms over his chest, making his shoulders appear as wide as the Texas landscape.

She swallowed the last of her pride. "Have you sent it to the papers yet?"

"Nope."

"Good. I mean, uh..." Her thoughts became scrambled

beneath the heat of his gaze. "I have an idea that you might want to consider. That is, if you're still interested."

He gave a slow nod. "It's warm today." He ran his hand down his chest. Sweat clung to his skin, making it shimmer in the sunlight.

Her pulse skittered.

"I could probably hunt us up something cool to drink. Come on in."

"Sure." She clasped her purse at her waist, feeling as awkward as a girl about to ask a boy to a Sadie Hawkins dance. "That'd be nice."

He walked up the steps in a slow, sauntering way that only a cowboy could manage. He pushed open the door and nodded for her to enter ahead of him. Doffing his hat, he hung it on a peg inside the door.

It took a moment for Elise's eyes to adjust from the bright sunlight to the dimness inside the house. Then her mouth opened with surprise. The entryway was wide and spacious—nothing fancy, but homey in a country-fashioned way, with warm colors of wheat fields and sunlit green pastures.

"Make yourself at home. I'll go throw on a shirt." He gave her a sheepish expression that caused a new heat wave to roll through her. "I wasn't expecting company. I was working down at the barn when I saw you drive up in...was that Chuck's Ford?"

Unable to formulate an answer, much less speak, she nodded. Her boss had let her borrow his truck a couple of times when she'd had doctor appointments. And he'd let her borrow it again today. No questions asked.

"I'll be right back." He turned and then pointed. "The kitchen's right through there."

Trying to forget the sight of his muscled back and the width of his shoulders, Elise turned in the way he'd pointed. She walked through a wood-paneled living area, complete with a beige sofa and television console. She glimpsed a wall of photographs but resisted the temptation to study them closely and went on, into the kitchen.

It was a sunny, cozy nook, with white-painted cabinets, clean counters and colorful pictures that Cole's daughter must have drawn stuck on the refrigerator. He'd described his home accurately—nothing elaborate, but tastefully decorated and downright homey. Her chest clenched with need and hope.

When she heard the sound of Cole's approaching footsteps, his boots clomping against the hardwood floors, she greeted him with a smile and a cold glass of ice water. "Since you've been working, I thought you might be thirsty."

"Thanks," he said, offering her a restrained smile in return. He downed the water in a few greedy gulps. The muscles along his throat mesmerized her. She had to shake off his effect on her. She wasn't interested in marrying Cole because of his obvious good looks. She simply wanted a home. Needed one. And if it came with a handsome husband, well, so much the better.

Together, they settled at the kitchen table. Cole straddled a chair and rested his elbows on the wooden table's edge. Elise sat demurely across from him, crossing her ankles, folding her hands tightly in her lap.

After he downed a second glass of water, he scratched his brow thoughtfully. "Did you think of something else we should add?"

Panic arched through her. *Oh, God! What if he doesn't think I'm the right type to be a wife? Like Rusty. What if Cole doesn't believe I'm good enough to be a mother to his daughter?*

Her heart pounded with dread. But she ignored the

doubts spinning through her head. She wasn't going to sit back and wait as she'd done her whole life. She had to take the bull by the horns, so to speak, and get on with her life, make a future for herself. Here was an opportunity she couldn't pass up.

"No, I think the copy for the ad was just right. In fact, it was so perfect, that I started thinking..." She swallowed the hard lump in her throat.

"About...?" His steady gaze made her stomach flutter.

"About..." Her voice squeaked. Clearing her throat, she tried again. "That I might...that maybe you'd consider..." *Oh, God, she was bungling this for sure.* "I'd like to volunteer—" she gritted her teeth and forced herself to say the words that were sticking in her throat "—to be your mail-order bride."

Elise could hear the blood pumping through her veins, echoing in her ears. Her face burned. She wished she could sink right through the floor. She felt like she was seven years old again, standing before a couple who'd come to look her over—who'd given the slight shake of their heads that she didn't measure up. She wasn't good enough to be their daughter.

A sharp need sliced through her heart. She wanted to bolt right out of her chair and race for Chuck's pickup before she suffered the same humiliation by Cole. But she planted her feet firmly on the floor. Not this time. This time it was too important. This time it wasn't just her pride, it was her life on the line. She clenched her hands into fists and lifted her chin, defying him to laugh at her.

But he didn't. Instead, Cole eased back in his chair, clasping his hands over his taut abdomen. His blue eyes narrowed to slits. "Why?"

"Why?" she repeated, uncertainty invading her once again. She shifted in her seat, recrossed her ankles, clutched her hands together, trying to stop the trembling inside her.

He tapped his thumbs together with a slow, deliberate beat, as if counting the seconds, making her heart race. "Why would you be interested in living here, way out in the country, mothering a child you don't know? Marrying a man you don't love?"

She found her voice and a new strength inside her that she hadn't known existed before now. "It's simple." Or so she'd thought at one time. "I'm pregnant."

Chapter Two

If a rabbit had hopped out of his Stetson, Cole wouldn't have been more surprised. He blinked once, twice, letting Elise's statement sink in. Then he slid his gaze over her slim figure as she sat at his kitchen table. He noticed her full breasts beneath the lightweight cotton top, her flat stomach and her narrow, almost boyish, hips beneath the full, flowing skirt.

She didn't look pregnant. But then he wasn't an expert on women. Especially pregnant ones. He certainly didn't relish the idea of having another pregnant woman in his house. His ex-wife had been a nightmare to live with while she'd carried Haley. He couldn't—wouldn't—go through that again.

But Elise's confession piqued his curiosity and made him wonder what she truly wanted. Was it to marry him, have her baby, and then leave him with another burden, another responsibility, like his ex-wife had? The memory twisted his insides.

"How far along are you?" he asked, his shoulders

hunched forward as kinks formed along the tightening ridge of his spine.

"Three and a half months." She pressed her hand against her lower abdomen and a soft smile curled her lips, making his insides tighten with an interest he didn't want or need. "I haven't started to show much yet. But I can't wait to be big and round and start wearing maternity clothes."

His eyebrows arched with disbelief. His ex-wife certainly hadn't been thrilled with the prospect of gaining weight, having swollen feet or accumulating stretch marks. He'd taken the brunt of her anger as her body had changed over the long nine—actually nine and a half—months.

He stared at Elise for a full minute, pondering her statement, questioning whether he believed her or not. "You don't mind being pregnant?"

A smile bloomed across her face, transforming her ordinary freckled features into a work of art, worthy of a museum. It made her even more beautiful, more radiant than before. He had a hard time concentrating on his need to give her a resounding "no."

A tightness twisted his chest, and a lump formed in his throat. Damn. He could picture her in his mind's eye with a softly rounded belly, her auburn hair teasing her shoulders and that same heart-warming smile that reached her eyes and his heart. He imagined what it would be like to hold her, to feel her soft curves melt against him and taste her full lips.

Whoa! What the hell am I doing? Putting the cart way ahead of the horse. She's pregnant, for God's sake! He reminded himself again and again until the appealing image vanished beneath an onslaught of painful memories.

It didn't matter if he was attracted to her. When she'd first admitted her reason for coming to his ranch today, he'd felt a quickening of his pulse. He'd thought his luck was turning. He had hoped the woman who volunteered to be his mail-order bride would be attractive. But it wasn't a requirement. It was a bonus. And he'd felt damn lucky all of a sudden.

Then she'd hit him with news that was like a donkey kick to the gut. He felt the impact shattering his hope like glass. It did matter that Elise was pregnant. It mattered a lot.

Now what the hell was he going to do about her proposal?

"Oh, yes!" she exclaimed. "I love being pregnant. I don't even mind the nausea." She smoothed her hand over her abdomen in a protective gesture, as if guarding the baby growing inside her. Paula had never acted maternal during or after her pregnancy. Nothing could have prepared Cole for the remarkable difference he saw in Elise. And the response it provoked inside him.

"But I never thought," she added, "I'd be single and pregnant. That wasn't in my plans."

He knew all about failed plans. Watching Elise, he had an urge to move closer to her, to wrap a protective arm around her, to... He stopped himself again. His mind spun with questions, not only aimed at Elise but also at himself. *If* he were to marry her, and that was a big *if,* then he'd have more than the added responsibility of a wife. He'd have another child. Another mouth to feed. A truckload of new responsibilities.

My God, what am I doing? Was he actually contemplating the possibility of marrying this unwed mother-to-be?

Drawing in a steadying breath, he asked, "Do you know who the father is?"

Her shoulders jerked, and a spark ignited in her hazel

eyes, making them blaze with defiance. "Of course! What kind of a woman do you think I am?"

He shrugged. Hell, he didn't know her past, her character, morals or even her plans for the future. He certainly didn't know if she was the type of woman he wanted influencing his impressionable daughter. Why, the father of her baby might be any one of a dozen men! "I don't know."

Her mouth opened and then closed abruptly into a thin, disapproving line. She lowered her eyes and smoothed her palms over her skirt. Her hands trembled.

"I suppose that's true." An inner strength fortified her voice, making it stronger and steadier than she looked. "I had an opportunity to question you the other day. I guess it's your turn. You have a right to know what you're getting yourself into. So go ahead. Ask any question you'd like."

Given the okay to pry into her personal life, he asked, "Where is the father?"

"I'm not sure at the moment. Rusty wasn't interested in being a father or in settling down so he moved on." She shook her head slightly, dismayed by her own circumstances. "He's on the rodeo circuit." She gave a soft, disbelieving chuckle. "I thought that sounded romantic once. I thought it was a traditional kind of profession. You know, handed down from father to son, cowboy to cowboy, through the generations."

She sucked in a harsh breath. "Boy, was I wrong." Her hands twisted in her lap, her fingers tightening on each other. "I also thought I was in love." Her voice softened, but the tension in her coiled like a steel spring, making her features look stark and pale. "Maybe I was in love with the idea of love. I naively followed him to a few rodeos. We were headed to Amarillo when I discovered I was pregnant. That's how I ended up in Desert Springs."

"He just left you here?" Cole asked, his blood pressure spiking with disbelief.

Elise nodded. "Without a cent or a way to—"

She stopped herself and her lashes shuttered her eyes, hiding her emotions from Cole. A bright red hue stole up her neck and deepened the color on her cheeks.

His hands curled into fists. How could a man do that? How could a man live with himself after walking away from the woman who carried his child?

He remembered the day Paula had told him they were going to have a baby. It seemed so long ago and yet it was as clear to him as the west Texas sky. Paula had been furious, angry...at *him*. But he'd been ecstatic, elated, joyous. He'd never known such euphoria. He'd wanted to shout from the nearest mountain top...er, plateau. He'd felt like the king of the world. Wanting to share the special moment with his wife, he'd tried to wrap his arms around her in a celebratory hug, but Paula had jerked away and thrown a vase at him.

Suddenly he felt a bond with Elise, one he'd never felt with his ex-wife. Elise had been rejected, as he had, as his daughter had. For some strange reason, he wanted to reassure her, to promise everything would be all right for her and her unborn child. But he resisted. He didn't know the whole story. Frankly, he didn't know what to do.

Still stunned that a man would behave in such a manner, he asked, "This Rusty fellow left you *after* you told him you were going to have his baby?"

"Yes. It became painfully apparent that he wasn't the man I'd thought he was." The quaver in her voice made Cole's gut clench with anger. "When he started to pack his bags, I didn't argue with him or try to stop him." She combed her fingers through her hair and sniffed daintily as if trying to forget the pain and the rejection she'd suffered. Then she lifted her chin, and her eyes burned with an inner fire of strength. "I let him go. I didn't want a man who didn't want me or my child. I wasn't going to grovel and beg."

He admired her convictions, her pride. But why was she turning to him? To a stranger for a husband? He sensed there was more to her story, more that she was leaving out.

"Don't you have family to turn to? Who can help you out?" he asked. Maybe her parents wouldn't approve of her being an unwed mother. Or maybe she was simply too embarrassed to return home.

Her chin jutted out once again. "I don't need anyone's help. I'm perfectly capable of caring for myself and my baby."

"But, then, why marry me?" he prodded. "Why would you want a loveless marriage?"

Her solid stare gave him a glimpse into her soul, a glimpse into dark and troubled waters. Part of him wanted to turn away. But another part of him, a nobler part, wanted to go to her.

"I wasn't out husband-hunting. In fact, I'd accepted the fact that I was going to be a single mom. Then I met you. Your reasons for wanting a wife made me start thinking. I want a family for my baby," she said, honesty ringing clearly in her voice. "I don't want my baby to grow up like—"

She broke off and glanced away. Her throat worked up and down for a moment as she wrestled with an inner demon. Cole had an urge to touch her, to comfort and console, but he resisted, not understanding the sudden need inside himself, and definitely not wanting any part of it.

* * *

When Elise had suppressed her out-of-control emotions, she added, "I want my baby to have both a mother and a father. A real home. Much like yourself, the way you want two parents for Haley."

Her gaze shifted away from Cole, from his intense stare that seemed to see right through her. She looked out the window. The peaceful quality she'd felt while driving onto his ranch had long since disappeared. Her nerves stretched tight as if they might snap at any moment. She knew Cole was the reason. She sensed his disapproval, his resistance. More than that, she realized she wanted this—his family, this home and Cole—more than anything. For her baby, of course.

She drew her bottom lip between her teeth. "I want my child to have a place to call his or her own. Roots that will help him or her to grow strong, confident and secure."

Her insides quaked. Had she said too much, revealed too much? She felt as vulnerable as if she stood before Cole naked, bare to his inspection, for him to see her flaws, mistakes, regrets and all. For him to judge her worthy or not.

"I see," he said after a lengthy, awkward pause.

"And you think I'd be a good father?"

"Yes," she said, meeting his gaze directly. Of that she felt certain. Her voice remained solid, without wavering, without doubts. Not that it made any sense, but she'd seen that special glow in his eyes when he'd spoken of his daughter. She'd heard his friends and neighbors talk about him with respect. But mostly because he'd do anything for his daughter's sake, including marrying a woman he didn't love. She understood that kind of sacrificial love. It was rare. And precious.

"How do you know? You haven't seen me with Haley." He crossed his arms over his chest. "I might be a horrible father. For her. For your baby."

Her breath caught in her throat. She knew what he was really saying. She felt as if she was on a roller coaster zooming down the last steep decline. "A horrible father wouldn't worry if his daughter was happy or not. Wouldn't set aside his ego, pride and desire to stay single when he realized his daughter needed a mother, too." She took a shaky breath. "If you were a horrible father, then you wouldn't have beamed when you spoke of your daughter."

A tremor started in her chest and spread to her limbs. She understood the doubts he'd expressed weren't about his ability to father, but about her ability to mother. She couldn't prove herself to him. Just like she hadn't been able to prove to the couples looking to adopt that she'd be a perfect match for their family. Feeling a sudden weight press against her chest, she grabbed her purse and stood, making the chair clatter behind her.

"Obviously you're not interested in marrying me." Anger and humiliation warred inside her. "I understand. Adding another child to the equation wasn't in your plans. So I thank you for your time, Cole. I'll be seeing you around town."

Forcing herself to walk and not run, she headed out of his house…away from the life she'd always dreamed of.

Dumbfounded, Cole watched her leave, unable to sort through his jumbled thoughts and form a response. Her words punched a hole through his doubts. He hoped he was a good father. He wanted to be. For Haley's sake. God, he'd tried. But he feared he would fail, as he'd failed in his marriage.

Elise had misunderstood him. He'd never thought of himself as a candidate for Father of the Year. He simply did what was necessary for his daughter, what he thought was best. Sometimes he'd been wrong. But in this case, in deciding to find Haley a mother, he knew as sure as lightning followed thunder that he'd made the right decision.

But was Elise the right woman for their family?

One thing he knew for certain—he wasn't ready for her to go. He hadn't made a decision. He didn't know what to do. Hell, he wasn't sure about every aspect of this crazy scheme he'd concocted. But he couldn't let her walk out, not like this. Racing to beat her to the front door, he called her name.

She faced him once more. "Good luck with your search for the perfect wife and mother."

With red-rimmed eyes and a determined jaw, she yanked open the front door.

"Wait, Elise!" Cole reached out and put a hand on her elbow. A frisson of electricity shocked him, scolded him for touching her again. But he realized in that instant that he wanted to draw her close and pull her against him. It made no sense, and he ignored the strange need. Carefully, he turned her to face him.

Tears brimmed in her eyes, unnerving him. Her wide, expectant gaze turned him inside out. Not knowing how to repair the damage he'd caused, he asked, "What did I say?"

She shook her head and sidestepped him, breaking the contact between them. She wrapped her arms across her middle. "It's what you didn't say. I threw a wrench into your well-thought-out plans. If you want to say no, then say it. Don't make excuses. I can take it."

"I didn't mean it as a rejection of you." He cupped both her elbows in his hands, pulled her closer. So close that he could smell her light perfume that seemed both to fog his head and sharpen his senses at once. "The thought of being a father again, to another baby, is scary."

"Or is it that you don't want to become a father to a baby who isn't yours?"

"It's definitely a consideration. It's a huge commitment."

"And marriage isn't?"

A wisp of a smile softened his stiff lips. "You're right. Maybe I thought it would be easier. I don't know."

Her gaze softened, and her features relaxed. "Where did you get the idea?"

He ran his fingers roughly through his hair and sucked in a breath. "My great-great-grandfather had a mail-order bride. Of course, I know it was during the eighteen hundreds. But they built the Double Heart Ranch together, had a huge family." He shrugged. "I figured love had failed for me during my first marriage, maybe something else might work better."

He stepped away, needing breathing room. Elise's understanding gaze unnerved him. He drew a thin stream of air into his tight lungs.

"Then, what is…" she asked, "…what's making your decision so difficult?"

He cursed beneath his breath, owning up to the fear that threatened to overwhelm him. "My wife left me and my daughter. I don't want that to happen again." He swung around and confronted Elise, anger pumping through his veins like oil through a rig. "Okay? How do I know that in three months' time you won't grow bored with this arrangement, with the ranch, with us? How do I know that you won't have the baby and leave your kid here while you go off to pursue…whatever?"

She met him toe-to-toe, propping her hands on her hips.

In a quiet, almost-still voice, she said, "Because I give you my word. Which is all I have to give.

"I'm not going to walk out on you, Cole Dalton. When I make a commitment, it's forever. I realize there are two little lives at stake here. I wouldn't do anything to harm your daughter or my baby. I certainly wouldn't desert my child." Her voice sounded strong and sure, in spite of the slight tremor.

Could he believe her? After all, Paula had promised to love, honor and cherish him, for better or worse. Worse had come sooner than better.

"This isn't an easy decision for me, either, Cole. I'm just as scared of being... I didn't make a rash decision before I came out this afternoon. Just as you didn't make a spur-of-the-moment decision to find yourself a wife. I've thought this through." She put her hand on his arm. Her warmth broke through the chill surrounding his heart, but his nerves cinched tight.

"But, Cole," she said, her gaze steady, her voice dipping low, "you still have questions. Take some time and think about it. Check out your other options. I'm sure there will be other women who'll jump at the chance to answer your advertisement."

"I don't know about that. As I said before, it's not you precisely that I'm questioning." It was his ability to trust versus his need to find a wife—and a mother for his daughter. He sucked in a breath and steadied his nerves. He felt a definite pull toward this intriguing woman who seemed to understand him better than he did himself. "Before we can decide anything, we need to conduct a test." His gaze settled on her inviting mouth.

She withdrew her hand from his arm. Her eyes widened. Her lips parted. "A test?"

He wanted to lean forward and kiss her, test the simmer

he felt each time they touched to see if it would boil. But that wasn't what was important now. Or was it?

Tension pulled at the corners of Elise's mouth. Her throat went bone dry. What did he mean?

She'd seen that look in a man's eyes. Desire. Plain and simple. The way it made Cole's eyes darken like a cloud bank of sin unnerved her. She felt his gaze move over her like a slow caress. The hair at the back of her neck prickled and a shimmy of anticipation—no, wariness—rippled down her spine. She stared at his wide, generous mouth, unsure if he made her nervous or if it was the scintillating thoughts churning inside her mind. "What kind of a test?"

"You need to meet Haley," he said, as cool and controlled as she was hot and uneasy. "If you get along, then maybe we can work something out."

It wasn't exactly a proposal to write home about. But then she didn't have a home. Or anyone to write to. What more could a woman like her ask for? "And if we don't..." she offered, squaring her shoulders, preparing herself for the inevitable rejection, "then I guess all bets are off."

He nodded. "I guess so."

An hour later, tension twisted her insides into constricting knots as she waited for Cole to return home with his daughter from school. Elise had never been good at taking tests or giving auditions. She was suffering from an acute case of performance anxiety.

How many times had she "performed" for wanna-be adoptive parents and failed? How many times had she been lacking whatever it was the adoptive couples wanted in their child. A boy? Blue eyes? Blond hair? The perfect smile? Top grades? She knew she'd set herself up for failure this time. After all, Haley probably didn't want just any mommy. She wanted her own. How could Elise compete?

Or maybe Cole had set her up for failure. Maybe he still wanted a way out of this deal without feeling like a bad guy. She couldn't blame him really. It was asking a lot for a stranger to take on the extra responsibility of a wife and new baby. Then again, it wasn't asking any more than he was requiring for his mail-order bride.

As she waited in Cole's living room, Elise sat on the edge of the sofa as if it might swallow her if she were to lean back and relax. She wondered if he'd been honest about his precious darling. Maybe Haley was a little tyrant. Maybe that's why he hadn't been able to keep even a nanny.

Worrying her lower lip, she tried to remember how she'd worked with the younger kids at the orphanage. The nuns had said she was a natural. Placing her hand over her abdomen, she hoped and prayed that was true. She wanted to be a wonderful mother for her baby. Trouble was, she had nobody to compare herself to, no role model, except for Mrs. Brady and Mrs. Cleaver on television.

The front door of Cole's house swung open and banged against a wall. Elise heard the patter of tiny feet and guessed little Haley was running or skipping, like most five year olds. She plastered on her best smile, straightened her shoulders and prepared to meet Cole's daughter. But she only caught a blur of bouncing blond curls as the little girl raced through the den and up the stairs.

The slamming of a distant door had Elise's spine stiffening. Something wasn't right. And *she* had to be the reason. The little girl had asked for a mommy in a weak moment, but when faced with the real possibility, Haley must have had visions of an evil stepmom, like in "Hansel and Gretel."

"Sorry about that." A weathered and weary-looking Cole stepped into the room and leaned against the door-jamb. The lines in his face looked deeper, starker, like cracks in granite. His eyes deepened to a dark, troubled blue.

"Guess she didn't like the idea of a stepmother." Elise clutched her purse in her lap and knew she'd met her match. There was no fighting a five year old who had her father wrapped around her little finger. She wouldn't blame Cole for wanting to back out now. Not when his daughter was obviously so upset by the idea.

He shook his head and combed his fingers through his short-cropped hair, about the hundredth time to do so in the last hour. "That's not it. She's upset at me."

Tension in her shoulders pinched her nerve endings. "Why?"

"I forgot about today."

Elise sank back against the sofa cushions and expelled a breath. She remembered crying herself to sleep when no one had remembered her sixteenth birthday. No square birthday cake with frosting flowers and candles. No presents. No nothing. She'd gotten over it eventually. Now it never bothered her that no one cared. It wasn't such a special day. "It's her birthday, isn't it?"

"No. I could never forget that date. But it was fairy tale day in her kindergarten class." He walked across the room, his motions stiff, as if with each step he punished himself. "I forgot all about it. Haley was the only one who didn't dress up like her favorite fairy-tale character."

"Oh, I see." Elise studied the distraught father and sensed his self-loathing.

"I have no idea how to make it better." He cursed beneath his breath, the words aimed like a rifle at himself. "If she'd skinned her knee, I'd know how to treat that."

"You've learned how to kiss boo-boos, eh?" Elise asked, trying to lighten the situation and her own somber mood. This wasn't as big a travesty as Cole thought.

"Dammit, I've broken her heart. How do I fix that?" The pain in his voice slapped at Elise.

A crack opened in her heart. No one had ever worried about her feelings. Yet this father acted like he'd committed a grievous sin against his little daughter. His reaction moved Elise in ways she'd never anticipated.

"Believe me," she said, sympathizing with Cole, "she'll get over this." She had a strange urge to go to him and wrap her arms around him. Instead, she crossed her arms over her middle. "All little girls have disappointments. And they survive. It's part of growing up. She'll forget all about this in time."

"I don't know. She's pretty upset. She cried all the way home." His ragged face told Elise how those childish tears had flooded his own heart.

His pain touched her soul, made her yearn for someone to care as much about her child—and her. "Maybe I can help," she offered, putting her purse on the sofa and rising. "I'll go talk to her."

He shifted, as if coming to attention. "I didn't tell her about you yet. I didn't have a chance."

"It's okay. I'll introduce myself and tell her I'm your new friend. Okay?"

"But what will you say? How can you fix things?" His brow bunched into a frown of despair.

She gave him a soft smile and put a hand on his warm, sturdy shoulder. A spark of electricity rippled up her arm and she jerked her hand away, unwilling and unable to consider anything other than friendship with him. But she did feel a bond forming, an understanding that only two parents could truly experience. "Don't worry. I'll take care of it."

Cole paced back and forth, along an imaginary worry line in the carpet. With each step he cursed himself for his stupidity. How could he have forgotten Haley's special day at school? How could he ever make it up to her?

As the minutes ticked slowly by he began to doubt the wisdom of sending Elise to clean up his mess. He was responsible. He should fix it. But how?

If Haley didn't take to Elise, then it could easily make matters worse. But he'd wanted to believe Elise could help. He'd been grateful that she'd offered. But should he have let her take charge? Maybe he should check on his daughter. He started to climb the stairs but stopped at the strange noise coming from Haley's bedroom. It sounded like...

He took a few more steps, two at a time, before he recognized giggling. Giggling! The infectious laughter set him back on his heels. He stared at the closed door and felt locked out of his daughter's life. Jealousy arched through him. What were they laughing about?

Why couldn't *he* have made Haley laugh? His insides twisted with raw disappointment.

It was true then. Haley needed a mother more than she needed him. He felt his heart collapse beneath the weight of that reality.

Slowly he descended the stairs and returned to the den. He sank onto the sofa, propped his elbows on his knees and dug his fingers through his hair in frustration. His head throbbed. His chest ached with a pain he could only ascribe to the trials and tribulations of parenthood.

Suddenly he heard the door to Haley's room open. He jerked upright and sat back on the couch, trying to pretend he wasn't concerned, that it didn't hurt like hell that his daughter needed someone other than him.

When Haley practically skipped down the stairs, a smile had replaced her quivering chin and the tears from earlier. Amazed at the transformation, he watched her twirl across the floor, showing off the fancy dress her mother had sent two weeks after her last birthday, the one that was as inappropriate for a ranch as Paula herself had been. The dress had yards and yards of pink ruffles and white lace. Haley looked like a little parasol, her full skirt sailing outward and dipping inward as she turned around and around.

Giggling, she said, "Hi, Daddy!"

"Don't you look beautiful!" His smile turned genuine. His chest swelled with pride and love, blocking out the jealousy and pain he'd felt earlier. He didn't care what made his daughter happy, as long as she was.

Behind his daughter, Elise entered the room and gave him a subtle wink that made his blood pressure escalate.

"Elise says I look like Goldilocks." She patted her soft curls and gave another twirl. "But I want to be Cinderella. Do I look like a fairy-tale princess, Daddy?"

He noticed then that she wore a makeshift cardboard crown on the top of her head. The cardboard had been sprinkled with silver glitter.

"All you need is a pumpkin turned into a coach," he said, suddenly grateful to Elise and the magic she'd worked on his daughter, like a true fairy godmother. "And little mice scampering at your feet."

"Don't forget," Elise chimed in, her gaze settling on him, making his clothes feel suddenly too tight, "Prince Charming."

"That's you, Daddy." Haley crawled up into his lap, her dress rustling, and circled her arms around his neck.

He gathered her close and felt his chest constrict. Over

the top of his daughter's downy head, he whispered to Elise, "Thank you."

She gave a slight nod of understanding, blinked suddenly and turned away.

"Elise said I could wear my costume tomorrow. That I'd be the only fairy princess at school. That everybody would notice me. If I'd worn it today, then I would've gotten lost in the crowd. Can I, Daddy? Can I?"

"Of course, darlin'." He kissed her round cheek but his gaze remained on Elise. This woman had conjured up a miracle.

Maybe this wasn't such a far-fetched scheme. Maybe a marriage, for convenience sake, could work. With the right woman, of course.

Was Elise that woman? He was beginning to think she was. Not only did she get along great with Haley, but she was attractive, more beautiful than he'd hoped for. His future suddenly looked brighter.

Even the marriage bed offered new possibilities.

Chapter Three

"Will you marry me?"

Elise stared at Cole for a long moment. It wasn't the proposal she'd always imagined. No bent knee. No promised words of love. No engagement ring, even.

She reminded herself that this was more of a business arrangement—an agreement made between two consenting adults for the benefit of their children, not a heartfelt act. Still, something inside her constricted, ached with a resonance she couldn't explain and didn't want to analyze.

Oh, come on, Elise! You can't have everything. Here's a man, a strong, good-looking man who has a home and a family, asking to marry you. And he's willing to offer it all to you! Just not love. Don't believe in fairy tales. This is your reality. It's all a woman like you can hope for.

Cole walked toward her and grasped her hands in his much larger ones. Electricity skittered through her, making her feel as if every nerve was exposed. His eyes darkened, turned to a misty blue-gray. "Are *you* having doubts now?"

The roughness and uncertainty in his voice took hold of her heart and squeezed it tight. Slowly she shook her head and pushed away the pain that she'd never have a Cinderella wedding, never have that fairy tale ending.

This was as good as it would get.

She wouldn't bypass such a wonderful opportunity for her baby. Her unborn child was the most important factor for her to consider. Not her heart.

"No, no second thoughts," she said, and then tried to press her lips into a semblance of a smile. "Or cold feet."

"So—" he prodded.

"Yes, I'll marry you, Cole." The words tasted strange in her mouth. Heat surged through her veins, making her nerve endings spark as if they'd been set on fire. Acidic tears burned the backs of her eyes.

His features softened for a moment, and her abdomen rippled in response. Then he stepped away, releasing his grip on her hands. A chill whipped through her, as doubts swirled around her mind. *Oh, God! What have I done?*

"Then it's settled." He shoved his hands into his back pockets as if uncertain what to do or say now that the decision had been made.

She knew exactly how he felt. Her insides quaked with finality. A nervous energy made her jittery. She felt as if she was hanging by her fingertips off a cliff. Was Cole the one pulling her up to safety? Or was he pushing her over the edge?

Her stomach plummeted, and she felt an overwhelming need to bawl. It had to be hormones. Or was she making a mistake she'd regret for the rest of her life?

"So when do you want to tie the knot?" he asked.

Unwilling to back away from what she'd always wanted and now needed more than ever, she managed to say, "The sooner the better."

He nodded. "We better make it official before you start showing."

"Yes." Awkwardness wrapped around them like barbed wire, poking at them, pushing them together, and keeping them apart, making Elise feel totally exposed.

"How about this weekend? We could get a justice of the peace to perform the ceremony." His mouth thinned. "Or were you hoping for a church wedding?"

Emotions she didn't want to face clogged her throat. Of course she wanted a church wedding, the kind all women dreamed of, with a frilly white dress, fragrant flowers and a handsome groom. She wanted to be surrounded by family and friends at a pull-out-the-stops reception with a three-tiered cake and champagne that would make her as dizzy as her groom's kisses made her. But it wasn't meant to be. She'd have to settle for a sexy cowboy groom. And that was all.

"A justice of the peace will be fine."

"Good." He actually looked relieved, and she felt a twinge of disappointment. "I'll take care of the details. Why don't we plan to do it on Saturday? I'll even get the witnesses."

"Fine." She didn't know many folks here anyway. Who would she invite? She had no family, no friends. No one. Reality stung her heart.

"Would you like to invite your folks?" he asked. "Mine are gone now, but I'd be glad to bring yours in for the wedding."

"My parents?" she asked, her throat shutting down. She shook her head. "No, they wouldn't come."

She then realized there was one condition she hadn't made clear. And she needed to do so immediately. Before Cole got the wrong impression.

"Cole?" she said, feeling nausea wash over her. She

blamed it on her pregnancy and not on her nerves. She swallowed hard before proceeding. "There's something we haven't discussed."

His brow lifted, and he waited silently for her to continue. His blue eyes studied her intently, made her insides feel like hot, melted wax.

She looked away in order to strengthen herself and compose her thoughts. "This marriage...well...it's going to be in name only."

Slanting her gaze toward him, she wondered if he understood. He didn't move, blink or respond. He simply stood there with a blank look on his chiseled face, as if trying to understand.

"I mean," she said, her courage wavering, "there won't be any..." She cleared her throat and dove into the hot topic. "...sex."

Cole felt the surrounding walls close in on him, suffocating, locking around him like a jail cell. He hadn't expected her to jump into bed with him the first night. He'd just assumed after a while they'd form a real marriage.

Okay, he admitted only to himself, he'd started to anticipate making love to Elise. Hell, he was a normal red-blooded American male. And it had been way too long since he'd been intimate with a woman. Now, dammit, it might be even longer! Did she want him to be celibate for the rest of his life?

Looking at the firm resolve in her hazel eyes and squared chin, he knew she was serious, and that she wouldn't back down. His shoulders tensed. His stomach dropped like a brick. He tried to imagine a lifetime of no sex. A marriage without a marriage bed.

Good God, she couldn't be serious!

Okay, he realized, getting a mail-order bride wasn't as easy near the turn of this century as it was at the turn of the last for his great-great-grandfather in the eighteen hundreds. He doubted Jessie Dalton's bride had set Elise's stringent condition. Or if she had, she hadn't stuck to it for long. After all, they'd had twelve children, the first arriving on their one-year anniversary. Cole knew better than to believe the stork had delivered that baby boy.

He sucked in a steadying breath and tried to release his sudden pent-up frustration. Maybe with time, Elise would relent. Or maybe she wouldn't. He couldn't count on that kind of possibility. Had she had a horrible experience with her ex-rodeo-cowboy? Had he hurt her?

Cole's hands folded into fists at the thought of another man touching Elise, bruising her pale skin. It was an irrational reaction. He was simply feeling protective toward her. That's all. Then why did the thought of never being able to touch or kiss her make his heart pound, sweat pop out on his forehead and his insides quake with disappointment?

Maybe it was her pregnancy that made her wary about making love. Or hormones making her not interested in sex. He clearly remembered Paula pushing him away, night after night, until he'd stopped approaching her. Good God! Was Elise going to end up like Paula after all?

"Did I surprise you?" Elise asked.

Cole ground his teeth. Why did her voice suddenly sound like liquid velvet? Maybe it was just his imagination running amok. Or his hormones.

Still dazed from her declaration, he shook his head. "I— I...no. I guess not. I should have anticipated it...or some form of it."

She crossed her arms over her chest. "You didn't expect me to go to bed with a complete stranger, did you?"

"I really hadn't thought about." Although he admitted only to himself he'd imagined what it would be like to kiss Elise, to hold her, to lie in bed with her snuggled against his side. Now, he'd never know.

Feeling like a corralled bull with a field full of heifers on the other side of a tall, well-built fence, he paced a few steps away from her. He tried to work out the kinks tightening his muscles but each second twisted the knots like a screwdriver. Finally he faced her again. "I didn't think we'd consummate the relationship immediately. I thought after a while, when we got to know each other, when we were more comfortable…" He plowed his fingers through his hair. What *had* he been thinking? "I don't know."

"Can you live with that condition?" she asked, her brow wrinkling with concern.

He really had no choice. Not if he wanted a mother for his daughter. That was the reason for the marriage anyway, not to satisfy his own selfish needs. Elise certainly seemed like the right candidate to mother Haley. But the thought of never touching Elise made him almost groan out loud.

"Let's reevaluate this in six months."

"What will that accomplish?" she asked, defiant.

"You might feel differently when you're no longer pregnant."

"I doubt it. But I understand your…um…concerns."

Did she really?

"I'm not making any promises, Cole."

"I understand that." Maybe she was shy. After all, her boyfriend just recently dumped her. She simply needed time. "Here's my one condition in return."

She noticeably stiffened in response. Her shoulders squared and her chin lifted. "What's that?"

"That everyone else believe this is a real marriage in every sense of the word. I don't want it getting back to my daughter that it's only a marriage of convenience. I don't think that would be healthy. We'll have to at least appear to be a happy, *loving* couple. Can *you* live with that?''

She took a long time contemplating the idea. His stomach churned. His forehead compressed into a frown as tension weighed down his shoulders.

Finally, she gave a slight nod and reached out her hand. ''It's a deal.''

He took her hand in his, felt the silky softness of her palm rub against him. Her fingers clasped his hand without an ounce of shyness or reserve, and her heat wrapped around him, made him want...need.... Desire reared its ugly head again. Damn, he was about to spend the next six months taking cold showers.

It was a sun-drenched day. A perfect day for a spring wedding. A day that conjured up images of beautiful white doves and blossoming love. But Elise didn't feel giddy or elated, as a bride should. She felt as if her nerves were exposed to the raw and edgy elements of the outside world.

She gave one more glance to the mirror above the dresser and realized the narrow skirt she'd bought for this day wouldn't button much longer. She tugged one last time at the off-white satin jacket. The flare of material around her narrow hips helped cover the soft roundness of her tummy.

''You look purty,'' Haley said, standing behind her in her pink ruffled Cinderella dress. ''Like a fairy princess!''

''Thanks, honey.'' Elise tucked her hand under the little girl's chin and gave an affectionate squeeze. ''So do you.''

''Can I wear my crown?'' Haley asked.

''If you'd like. Want me to pin it on top of your head?''

The little girl grinned and nodded. After a few moments of wrestling with bobby pins, Elise stood back, patted the girl's blond halo of curls and said, "You look like a bride yourself."

Haley gave her a toothy grin. "Is Daddy your Prince Charming?"

Stunned, Elise couldn't push an answer past the sudden lump in her throat. Her heart compressed with the weight of lost hopes and dreams. She thought of Cole, his bright blue eyes, the creases surrounding his mouth, his powerful hands that had touched her, moved her, unnerved her. With his black Stetson, faded blue jeans and hard, muscular chest, he didn't resemble any prince she'd ever imagined. But then, in a way, he *had* rescued her.

Somehow, that thought made her uneasy and yet at the same time gave her a sense of calm longing. She'd never thought of herself as a damsel in distress needing a knight in shining armor. But maybe she was. He certainly had presented a tempting offer she hadn't been able to refuse.

"Yes, darling, I guess your daddy is my Prince Charming." She gave a tentative smile.

Haley placed her hand, and trust, in Elise's, startling her, making her heart swell.

Fighting back a flood of emotions she couldn't explain away, Elise cleared her throat. "We better go downstairs. Your daddy is waiting."

Haley skipped toward the door, pulling Elise with her. "I think Uncle Jack and Aunt MaryAnn are here."

"Good, then it's almost time to leave." Elise swallowed the rest of her reservations, tightened her grip on her unraveled nerves and held onto Haley's warm, accepting hand.

"You're gonna be my new momma. Daddy said so!" Haley walked alongside Elise as they headed down the stairs to meet Cole's best friend and his wife.

A million questions and doubts made her feel as if she

were walking through quicksand. What if Jack and
MaryAnn could see right through the charade? What if
they asked too many questions? What if they disapproved
of Cole's choice of a bride? Her knees began to shake.

She heard a rumble of voices as she rounded the last
corner. When she entered the den, the conversation came
to an abrupt halt, as if she'd walked in at an inappropriate
time. Her skin electrified. Had they been discussing her?

Elise's gaze immediately sought out Cole for reassurance. But the sight of him snagged her breath in her throat.
Her breasts tightened with awareness.

He looked like the Marlboro man wearing a rented tuxedo. The black jacket, together with Cole's dark hair, made
his eyes stand out like neon lights. Elise felt her stomach
roll with admiration and pride. There might never be love
in their marriage, but she'd certainly caught herself a handsome husband.

Cole's bold gaze settled on her, widening with approval.
Her stomach plunged like an anchor finding the ocean
floor. What had she made him agree to? That he'd never
touch or kiss her? Was she nuts?

Wary of the feelings stirring inside her, she shook off
the sudden desire to go to him, to feel his strength beside
her. Hadn't similar feelings gotten her in this predicament
in the first place? She'd made a fool of herself once for
the sake of what she'd thought was love. Never again.

She decided the flutter in her stomach was the baby or
morning sickness. That was all. That was something she
could live with.

A low whistle shattered the silence in the room. "Jeez,
Cole," declared the man standing beside the groom, giving
Elise a broad, cheerful grin. "You didn't tell us how beau-
tiful your bride-to-be is?"

"Didn't I?" Cole looked stunned, as if he'd been zapped by a bolt of lightning.

"Well, don't just stand there with your tongue hanging out of your mouth. Introduce us!" The man slapped Cole on the back.

Cole stepped forward and held out his hand for Elise to take. She hesitated, doubts twisting around her spine like poison oak. Tentatively, she placed her hand in his and moved toward him. His hand felt warm and comforting even as tiny sparks ignited along her nerve endings.

"You do look beautiful," Cole said, his voice deep and penetrating, making her insides shake.

"So do you," she said. Heat burned her neck and cheeks.

A woman's laughter erupted nearby. "This is so romantic! So exciting!" The bleached blonde moved forward, embraced Elise in a quick hug and whispered, "You've got yourself a wonderful man. Congratulations. Jack and I hope you'll be very happy."

Surprised by the woman's enthusiastic greeting, Elise floundered for a response but felt too overwhelmed to trust her own voice. And too distracted by Cole holding her hand to think clearly.

"That's MaryAnn," Cole said. "And this is her husband, Jack Gardener. We've been friends longer than we've been driving pickups."

"How long have you and Cole been seeing each other?" MaryAnn inquired, looping her arm through her husband's.

Elise tensed and looked toward Cole for help. "Not long," she said. "It's all been sort of…a whirlwind."

MaryAnn patted Elise's arm. "Well, I don't doubt that Cole could sweep a girl off her feet. Sometimes it doesn't take more than a glance before you know. With Jack and me, it took a lot longer, since we all grew up together. I had to wait for him to get out of that obnoxious teenager stage before he noticed anything besides bulls and broncs."

"But once I did," Jack said, "I was plumb loco over her."

Playfully, MaryAnn slapped her husband's lapel. "I almost had to hog-tie him to get him down the aisle." She chuckled and gave Elise a wink. "I can tell you certainly captured Cole's attention."

Cole cleared his throat, and Elise felt the rumble in his chest vibrate inside her. "I guess we'd better be off." He glanced at the mantle clock. "We're supposed to be there at two."

"You'll probably have to pull Judge Wright off the lake," Jack laughed. "He won't care if you're late or not, long as you don't disturb his fishing. Don't get me wrong. He's a good ol' boy. You don't mind a little fishy smell during your wedding, do you, Elise? If you're lucky, he'll give you a couple of catfish for your wedding dinner."

"That's enough, Jack," Cole growled.

"Oh, let me snap a picture first," MaryAnn said, reaching for her automatic camera. "You three stand there and smile pretty. This is an occasion we don't ever want to forget."

Cole wrapped his arm around Elise's waist, his fingers pressing into her sensitized flesh. She felt a flame of awareness. Her insides sizzled.

Then he reached for his daughter's hand and placed her against his other side. For a moment Elise felt her feet glued to that one spot, and tears clogged her throat. She'd never been a part of a family, real or imagined. And she wasn't a part of this one—yet. But hope sprang within her like spring's first blossom pushing through the last crusty patch of snow.

"Everybody say 'happily ever after' on three," Mary-Ann said.

Cole glanced at Elise then. His easy smile turned to concern. His hand tightened against her waist. "Are you okay?"

She nodded, unable to speak, unwilling to let the feeling escape. She wanted to stand here for the rest of her life, with Cole's arm around her, Haley standing on the other side of him and her baby nestled snugly in her abdomen. This is what she'd dreamed of for so long. She prayed it would last.

Surrounded by familiar faces, Cole felt as if he was sleepwalking through the wedding. Questions and doubts rolled around in his brain like jumbled dreams. A wintry numbness settled over him. He had a sudden urge to run.

With that damn condition of no sex hanging around his neck like a noose, he wished Elise had buck teeth and thin straggly hair instead of a beautiful smile, and that lush, long, auburn hair that his fingers itched to sift through. What the hell was he doing?

Feeling as if he were a teenager about to go to the prom, he handed her a bouquet of white roses. Her hazel eyes widened and then suddenly filled with tears. Before he could respond, before he could touch her soft, creamy cheek, she looked away. When she glanced back at him, she'd composed herself, hiding all emotions behind a gracious smile.

"Thank you," she whispered.

"My pleasure."

Without looking directly into her dazzling greenish-brown eyes, Cole straightened his tuxedo that felt more like a straitjacket and turned his gaze toward Judge Wright who was decked out in his fishing overalls. His rod and reel leaned against the wall behind him. Jack hadn't lied when he'd mentioned the fishy smell, either.

Mrs. Wright finished her rendition of the wedding march on the upright piano, and the room fell into silence. Cole could hear the pounding of his heart, Elise's shallow breaths and his daughter's dress rustling as she shifted from foot to foot. This was going to be his family. For better or worse.

"We're gathered here today," Judge Wright began, puffing out his chest in his official capacity, "to join these two young folks in the bonds of holy matrimony. These vows are not to be taken lightly."

As if transported through time, Cole remembered another day, a fancy church wedding and a similar monologue. He'd been in love then. But not anymore. Now he knew marriage took more than heart-palpitating, hormone-surging love. It took unwavering commitment and rock-solid determination. That was all he had, now. And he hoped it was what Elise was willing to give, too.

He wondered if his great-great-grandfather had felt the same way about his bride on the day of their wedding over a hundred years ago. Or had he fallen in love instantly?

Cole resisted that thought. A hard-nosed, sun-bronzed rancher who could survive the Texas wilderness wouldn't fall victim to such an emotion. And neither would Cole.

He felt a sharp pang of regret that he wouldn't have any more kids. Haley would be his only child. But he'd treat Elise's baby as his own. He wondered what it would be— a girl or boy. It made no difference to him. As long as they all bonded as a family.

He was no longer listening to the words the judge spoke. Instead, his mind drifted down paths and walkways toward the future. What would it be like to have a woman in the house again? Would Elise be as persnickety as Paula had been? As demanding? Remembering Elise's assertive statement that their marriage would be in name only, he knew she had her own set of ideals and rules that she lived by. Instead of irritating him, he actually admired her. But was admiration and banked desire enough?

"Cole?" The judge gave him a sharp look.

Jolted out of his thoughts, Cole said, "What?"

"Do you take this woman to be your wife?"

He looked at Elise then, at the softness in her eyes, at her proud forehead and stubborn jaw. Pride filled him. He doubted he could have done better finding a mother for Haley in a big metropolitan city. "Yes, uh-huh, I do."

The judge gave a nod and turned his steel-gray eyes to the bride. "Elise Margaret McConnell, do you take this man to be your lawfully wedded husband?"

"I do." She spoke softly but with firm conviction.

Cole glanced at her profile, studied the straight edge of her nose, the way her chin slanted upward, the curve of her jaw. He hoped they'd make a good team. If he could only temper his desire. But given time, and the daily routine of running a ranch, he was sure he'd get past this inexplicable need to touch and hold her. Or else he'd go crazy. Still, he held out hope that somehow he'd change her mind down the road. He would give her time to get through her pregnancy and adjust to married life.

"Do you have rings?" the judge asked.

"No," Elise said at the same moment Cole answered, "Yes, sir."

He fumbled in his pocket for the simple gold band he'd purchased yesterday in Amarillo. He'd thought about giving her the ring his mother had worn, the one handed down for five generations in his family—the one Paula had scoffed at. Then he'd thought better of it. This was enough for now. It stated she was his bride. That's all that was needed.

"But I didn't get you one," Elise said, with a quiver in her voice.

"Not a problem. I don't need one." He pulled the ring out of his pocket and placed it on her finger. Staring down at her hand, he noticed the slim tapered shape of her fingers, the smooth skin, the delicate veins branching out across the back of her hand. Feminine hands. Not pampered. But willing to work. He gave her hand a gentle, affectionate squeeze before releasing it and felt a tightness constrict his chest.

"Very well," the judge replied. "By the powers vested in me in this grand and glorious state of Texas, I declare you man and wife."

MaryAnn and Mrs. Wright sniffled into their handkerchiefs. Haley clapped her hands with glee, causing little bits of glitter to fall off her crown like fairy dust. The judge offered his congratulations.

Jack clapped Cole on the back. "Go ahead and kiss your bride, Dalton. What are you waiting for?"

"That's my line," the judge grumbled, but gave Cole the nod to proceed.

Feeling the tie around his neck tighten, Cole turned toward Elise, expecting her to bolt like a frightened filly. He placed his hands firmly on her waist. Staring down at her petal soft mouth he imagined what it would be like to taste her, to feel her open to him. God, he'd thought about it, dreamed about it most of last night. This might be his only opportunity to ever kiss her. It was the best excuse he could think of. And, dammit, he had to make it last—possibly a lifetime!

Chapter Four

This is not a good idea.

Elise could think of many activities wiser and safer than kissing Cole—like climbing Mount Everest during an avalanche.

Her gaze shifted, restlessly, nervously, from the judge to her groom. Cole's eyes burned with an intensity she could feel along her skin, as if she'd received a flash sunburn. A million reasons filed through her head on why she should put her hand against his chest and refuse to let him "kiss the bride," starting with her intense and irresistible attraction to him. How could she keep her emotions out of this marriage and her heart intact if she let him get too close, if she gave herself to him?

Only one thing stopped her from denying Cole the right to kiss her—their audience.

Judge Wright and his wife, along with Jack and MaryAnn Gardener, watched the bride and groom with joyful anticipation. But the pair of eyes that reminded Elise of the promise she'd made to Cole belonged to his five year-old daughter. Haley stared up at them, believing she had a new mommy, a complete family. And Elise wouldn't disappoint her.

Before she could collect herself, steel her nerves and protect her heart, Cole lifted his hand, accidentally grazing the side of her breast and eliciting a shimmy of electricity down her spine. He cupped her chin and angled his mouth over hers. In a warm breath that caressed her lips, he whispered her new name, "Mrs. Dalton."

An odd mixture of disappointment and amazement swelled in her throat. As a little girl she'd dreamed of being someone's wife. She'd wanted to belong to someone, to be sheltered and cherished. When Rusty walked out on her, she'd given up her dream. Now, she had the illusion, but not reality.

Cole didn't love her.

And she didn't love him.

Companionship would have to be enough.

But companionship wasn't on her mind when he covered her mouth with his. The rugged cowboy had a surprisingly gentle touch. His lips were softer than the hard line of his mouth would have suggested and reminded her of the potency of his smile. Slowly, with the mastery of a magician's sleight of hand, he coaxed her into responding, into kissing him back. Fully and completely she gave into the kiss.

He must have sensed her surrender because in that moment his arms enfolded her into his embrace, pulling her close against his solid chest. She could no longer concentrate on anything except his tender, yet commanding touch. The room spun around her. She clung to him for support, her senses aware of his clean masculine scent, his heat, his taste. Each nerve absorbed the impact of his kiss and vibrated as his mouth moved sensuously over hers. A surge of primal need radiated through her. He made her body burn for him and her heart yearn for something that could—or would—never be.

When his tongue tested the seam of her mouth, a bolt of awareness shocked her senses back to life. Stunned by her reaction, her desire to link her arms behind his neck and press herself against him, she pushed against his chest, straightening her elbows to put some much needed space between them.

Embarrassed by the heat firing her cheeks, Elise gave an inappropriate laugh, resembling a schoolgirl giggle, and pulled away. She avoided Cole's heavy-lidded gaze and ignored the reasons why fear pounded in her chest. She didn't want to give him the wrong impression. She had no intention of changing her mind about the marriage being in name only, now or in six months' time. She'd made her bed, so to speak, and she'd happily lie in it—alone.

Aware of the others watching them intently, she sighed dramatically to cover her panicked reaction. "Oh, Cole." Her breath came hard and fast. She sounded like a bad Marilyn Monroe imitator as she tried to regain her composure. "Can't you wait...till later?"

She hoped her flirtatious wink fooled the others and covered her uneasiness.

It didn't fool Cole. He'd felt the heat generated by their kiss. And he sensed her wariness now.

Damn him for losing his head. Damn him for kissing her. He should have ignored the traditional after-the-ceremony kiss. Elise probably thought it had been for show. For Jack, MaryAnn and the judge. But it hadn't. It had been for him.

Tonight would be the first of many cold showers he'd have to suffer over the next few months. Unless he could change Elise's mind and persuade her to consummate their marriage. He wouldn't survive if she held him at arm's length. He wanted her in his bed. The sooner the better.

"You'll have to wait," Jack said with a hearty laugh.

For six months or more. Cole gave himself a mental shake to shatter the staggering effect Elise's reluctant but surrendering kiss had on him. He shifted his attention to Jack. Cole's shoulders tensed. Could his best friend see through the charade of their marriage already?

"Judge Wright promised us some catfish," Jack continued, "and I aim to fry it at your place."

Relieved that his friend didn't suspect anything "fishy" with their marriage, Cole breathed easier.

"I sure did," the judge added, reaching for his rod and reel. "Best catfish in the state."

"Jack Gardener!" MaryAnn propped her hands on her hips. "You are the most unromantic man I've ever known."

Jack slipped an arm around his wife and pulled her close. "Just last night you were singing a different tune, darlin'."

Playfully, she tugged on his tie. "Oh, you!"

Jack kissed his wife soundly.

"Are we gonna have a wedding cake?" Haley asked, her big brown eyes glowing with excitement.

"Of course, sugar," MaryAnn stated. "I'll whip one up when we get back to your house."

Haley grinned, flashing her dimples and melting Cole's heart. "It's gotta have white frosting."

"Of course. It wouldn't be a real wedding cake if it didn't," MaryAnn agreed.

Cole tickled his daughter's side until she squirmed and giggled. "You little stinker, you can't fool me. You just want to lick the bowl."

"So do I," Elise added, giving Haley a conspiratorial wink.

Cole's gaze settled on his new bride. He knew he'd made the right decision. He couldn't explain it, but he sensed Elise would be a good mother to his daughter. Now, if he could just turn her into a full-fledged wife.

"You don't mind us staying for supper, do you, Cole?" MaryAnn asked softly.

"Not at all," Elise chimed in before he could answer. She twisted the gold band around her finger, and he understood she wasn't anxious to finally be alone with her groom. "We'd love to have you."

"Are you sure?" MaryAnn's eyebrows arched.

"Of course," Elise insisted, with a smile that couldn't hide her nervousness. She nodded, making a curl along her neck bob and sway enticingly. "Wouldn't we, Cole?"

"Uh, sure. Yeah." Then an idea hit him. The longer they had company the more time he and Elise would be forced to play the loving couple. Which would assure him ample opportunities to touch and kiss his new bride, hopefully tempting her with possibilities. Grinning, he added with more enthusiasm, "Yeah!"

Elise's eyes narrowed on him. He realized then he might be pushing his luck too far and would end up sleeping on the sofa.

Would they never leave?

Elise's eyes drooped with fatigue from the long, stressful day—her wedding day. Her limbs felt as heavy as Cole's iron skillet which MaryAnn had used to fry up the catfish in a tasty cornmeal batter. Elise sat on the worn beige sofa next to her husband. Cole had put his arm along the back of it when they'd first convened to the den with coffee and thick slices of wedding cake. She should have been getting used to him, having him so near, but with each touch or whispered kiss against her temple he continually tied her insides into knots. His daughter snuggled against his other side. Elise wished Haley would sit between them like a barricade.

Throughout the evening, Cole had taken every opportunity to touch Elise. He'd placed a hand on her waist, making her body hum. He'd clasped her hand and given her heart a jolt. He'd kissed her on the cheek, temple and even along the back of her neck which had nearly been her undoing. All, she assumed, for the benefit of their company.

Which she wished would leave.

As they sat on the couch avoiding questions about their own relationship and listening to Jack and MaryAnn argue about what they each remembered happening on their first date, Cole slipped his arm about Elise's shoulders. Her pulse skittered.

"I wouldn't have taken you out for a steak, MaryAnn." Jack sat in an armchair with his wife cross-legged on the floor between his feet and rubbed her neck. "Hell, I was a poor cowboy. I couldn't afford a steak dinner. We went for burgers."

"Why would I have worn that fancy blue dress with the sequins then, Jack?" MaryAnn flicked her hand against her husband's knee. "I bet you've got me confused with some other woman."

Elise felt her temperature spike as Cole's thumb caressed the curve of her upper arm. Tiny thrills arced down her spine. She resisted the urge to pull away.

"What color hair did I have back then?" MaryAnn asked, lifting her nose a notch as if she'd won this argument.

Cole laughed and his hand tightened on Elise's shoulder.

The tantalizing sensations made her squirm and Cole used the movement to settle her more firmly against his side. Her body felt stiff as if she'd been starched and ironed.

"How long have you two been married?" Elise asked.

"Seven years," Jack answered and grinned at his wife. "Right, honey?"

"Close enough. It'll be seven in five months," MaryAnn said.

"And do you have kids?" Elise asked, hoping to keep the conversation focused on them. And her mind off Cole.

"Not yet. But hopefully someday. That is, if Jack can remember what color hair I had when we first went out."

As the minutes ticked by, Cole's warmth and soft chuckle lulled her into a sense of security. She began to relax. Giving in to her weariness, she rested her head on his broad, sturdy shoulder. She had to admit he made a nice, comfortable pillow. The conversation swirled around her like a kaleidoscope.

"Damn." Jack shifted uneasily. "Hasn't your hair always been blond?"

Cole's chest rumbled with laughter beneath her cheek, mesmerizing her. She could hear the steady beat of his heart. It made her feel safe. Oh, so safe. When had she ever felt that way?

"Jack Gardener! You know this is not my natural hair color."

"Just take a wild guess, Jack," Cole said. "You're bound to lose anyway."

"Hell, I don't have to guess. I remember."

"You do not!" MaryAnn challenged.

The vibration of Cole's laughter stirred something inside Elise, something she didn't want to analyze. Resolutely, trying to block out her own feelings, she kept her eyes closed. *I'm not enjoying this. I'm simply tired.*

Her mind began to shut down and her pulse slowed. Her eyelids fluttered closed and she drifted into a different world. One where she was safe and protected and cherished.

"It was red."

"Auburn," MaryAnn corrected.

"Same thing," Jack grumbled.

"Ah, sugarlump," MaryAnn cooed, "you do remember."

"Don't call me that."

"Good thing the romance doesn't fade after so many years," Cole said with a chuckle. "Sugarlump, huh, big guy?"

"You tell a soul..." Jack's voice took on a feigned threat.

"Oh, dear!" MaryAnn's voice became a hushed whisper. "We've outstayed our welcome. Elise has conked out, and I bet Cole's just dying to carry his bride to bed."

Bed! Elise's eyes popped open. She jerked upright. Her spine felt as if a bolt of electricity had jarred her awake.

Cole placed a warm hand on her arm. "Guess it's that time. Right, honey?"

"Cole..." Elise warned. A flush of heat surged through her.

She imagined Cole's double bed. Or did he have a king-sized one? Her heart jack-hammered inside her chest. She didn't want to find out. Or did she?

What have I gotten myself into? Hadn't she made herself clear? They would *not* be sharing a bed. As soon as their guests left, she'd remind him of their agreement.

"Say no more." MaryAnn pushed to her feet, pulling her husband out of the chair. "Come on, sugarlump, let's go home."

Cole shifted his daughter in his arms and stood. Haley's

curly blond head lolled to the side, and then she awoke, startled. "It's okay, baby." He gently rubbed her back. "Time for bed."

Haley rubbed her eyes. One of her little hands settled on her father's muscled shoulder, making it look larger, stronger, more rugged than when Elise had used it as a pillow. She felt a tightness squeeze her chest. Someday he'd hold her baby the same way. She placed a protective hand over her abdomen. Her child would have a father, someone to lean on, someone to count on. Something she'd never had.

"Can Elise sleep with me?" Haley asked, her voice drawing the words out with her thick Texas accent.

"Not tonight, darlin'." Cole spoke in soothing tones that had the opposite effect on Elise.

"Why don't you come on home with us tonight, Haley?" MaryAnn patted the little girl's back. "We'd love to keep her overnight."

Haley tightened her arms around her daddy's neck and buried her face against his collar.

"She's all right here," Elise said, getting to her feet. Her mind spun with the possibility that she might be left alone with Cole—her new husband.

"We don't mind a bit." MaryAnn gave them a broad wink. "It'd give you lovebirds a little privacy. Y'all might want to work on producing a new li'l Dalton."

Elise's face burned. "No."

All eyes stared at her, watching and wondering.

"I mean..." she said, trying to cover her blunder. "Well, I, uh..."

"Actually," Cole interrupted, "it's a distinct possibility."

"Cole—" Then she saw the strange glint in his eyes. Was he pretending? Teasing? Paving the way for the big announcement that she was already pregnant? She snapped her mouth shut.

"It would be better for Haley if she stayed here. In her own home. In her own bed."

Elise agreed with Cole and looped one of Haley's curls around her finger. "This is such a big change for her. I don't want her to think that I'm coming between her and her father."

MaryAnn nodded. "I understand. But the offer stands for whenever you need…well, you know. A little time alone."

"Y'all should make some time for a real honeymoon," Jack added, clapping Cole on the back.

"We will." He gave Elise a hooded glance that made her knees weak. "In six months or so."

Her spine stiffened. "Yes, we were thinking of taking a family vacation. Maybe to Disney World."

Haley's eyes opened. "I wanna go, too."

"Of course, baby," Cole reassured his daughter. "But not tonight."

Haley snuggled against his shoulder. "Where are you gonna sleep, Elise?"

MaryAnn smirked and glanced at her husband with a knowing look. "Oh, sugar, Elise and your daddy are married now. They'll share a room. That's what old married folks do."

"Like real parents?" the little girl asked.

"Sure thing, darlin'." Cole gave his daughter a kiss on the forehead. "Elise is your new mommy. She's going to be living here from now on."

"If I have a bad dream, can I sleep with y'all?"

Cole's gaze shifted toward Elise. They'd never spoken of their sleeping arrangements. Other than agreeing they wouldn't "sleep" together.

Elise felt a tingle in the pit of her stomach.

"Any time, baby," Cole assured his daughter and made Elise nerves stretch taut. "Any time."

Okay, now what?

Cole could admit, at least to himself, that he hadn't thought through every aspect of this arrangement. Like where he should sleep. Or where Elise would sleep. And if that would be in the same room...the same bed.

He stared at the closed door to his bedroom and wondered what he was supposed to do now. He'd carried Elise's lone suitcase up the stairs and placed it on his wide bed. As he'd carted his daughter to her room, he'd heard Elise close the door behind him, shutting him out. He certainly couldn't blame her. But, damn. Now what?

He paced in front of the door, two steps one way, two steps back, but he always ended up in the same place with the same question. He couldn't insist they sleep together. Yet he couldn't sleep somewhere else. His daughter was notorious for getting up in the middle of the night. What would she think—or say to someone in town—if she found her daddy sleeping in the hallway, on the sofa downstairs or even in another bedroom. Nope, that wouldn't do. It would defeat the purpose of this marriage and Elise's promise to make it *appear* real.

Squaring his shoulders he took a deep breath. He didn't have a choice. He took a step toward the door and raised his hand. *Here goes.* He rapped his knuckles against the wood.

He waited.

Elise didn't answer.

Frowning, he knocked again. Again, she didn't respond. Was she already asleep? He glanced at the base of the door and noted the light. Unless she slept with the lights on, he felt sure she was awake. Was she ignoring him?

"Elise?" he whispered, not wanting to wake his daughter who was sleeping down the hall. "Elise, we need to talk."

The door swung open a half inch. One of her sharp hazel eyes met his curious gaze. "About what?"

"This is my room."

A long pause met his statement. Finally, she opened the door wider. He caught a glimpse of a T-shirt that skimmed her thighs and revealed her long, shapely legs. His gaze slid down them landing on her small, bare feet. His gut clenched. How was he *not* supposed to want to sleep with her when she looked like that? Okay, she hadn't made him promise not to want her.

If there was a place called hell, he was about to visit it.

She crossed her arms over her chest. "I didn't ask to stay in here. We had an agreement. You promised—"

"Yes. I know." Boy, did he! He kept his eyes on her face, avoiding her soft curves hiding beneath the nightshirt. "But Haley thinks we're staying in the same room like real parents."

Her mouth caught his attention as she drew her bottom lip between her teeth. He remembered the kiss they'd shared after they'd promised to love and honor—till death do they part. Tonight might be the death of him.

Keeping his thoughts on his daughter, where they belonged, he remembered having to explain to Haley that her mother had left, gone away, for good. She'd looked up at him with those solemn brown eyes and said, "Why? What did we do wrong?" He never wanted to feel that raw, aching hurt for his child again. He never wanted to wake up and find a brief note on the kitchen table that read, "Goodbye, Cole. Have a nice life."

His determination doubled as he met Elise's gaze square on. "You made a promise yourself. You agreed to make this marriage *look* real."

Elise narrowed her eyes. Then she shoved open the door with one hand. "Fine. But let me make one thing clear. I am not going to have sex with you. So stay on your side of the bed. I've taken a class in karate. Understand?"

He grinned. She had spunk. He'd always admired that in a woman. His ex-wife hadn't been tough enough to survive out here. He took a step into the room and paused only a breath away from her. He could have bent his head and captured that sweet mouth once more. But he resisted.

Instead, he said, "Where did you learn to kiss? Did you take a class for that, too?"

Any response Elise might have made lodged in her throat. With him standing so close, he made her thoughts tumble over themselves. She could smell his spicy cologne that conjured up a memory of warm lips taking hers. Her stomach tilted off center.

Perturbed with herself—for being in this situation as much as her response to him—she turned on her bare heel and strode across the room to the bed. Glaring at him, not taking her eyes off him for even a moment, she flung back the comforter. "Which side do you sleep on?"

"I'm used to sleeping alone. I don't stay on one side."

She swallowed a hard lump in her throat as she imagined Cole's leg or arm sneaking across to her side of the bed during the night and brushing against her. *Oh, God! What if he slept in the nude?*

"Well," she said, unable to find the words to voice that particular concern, "pick one."

He gave a slight nod in her direction. "Ladies first."

Gritting her teeth, she climbed into the bed, laid flat on her back and pulled the covers up to her chin. She followed

Cole's every movement as he came farther into the room and walked the length of the bed. Anticipating him crawling in beside her, she shifted closer to the edge until she thought if she breathed too deeply she'd fall off onto the floor.

Without a warning, he shut off the lights. Darkness swelled around her, engulfed her, and gave her heart a jolt. Her senses went on alert. She blinked, trying to make out Cole's shape as he moved around the room. Her ears strained to hear, over the thudding of her heart. She heard the rustle of material. Then the rasp of a zipper.

Oh, God!

Her breath caught in her throat. Panic inched up her spine. An image sprang to mind reminding her of his sunbronzed bare chest. With a sweaty grip she clutched the covers. She waited for his weight to shift the bed. She waited for him to make some remark, something to set her more on edge. She waited for his touch—part of her hoping, welcoming it, part of her praying he wouldn't dare.

She tried to remember something she'd learned in the self-defense class she'd taken a few years back. Her mind went blank. But she knew if he made a move toward her, she'd kick his butt out of bed and onto the floor without breaking a sweat. At least she hoped she would.

The moments passed in silence with only the rush of blood pounding in her ears. Finally, she heard the creak of a floorboard and a softly muffled grunt. She lifted her head off the pillow. The horizontal blinds cut the moonbeams into pieces as they slanted through the window and onto the floor. In the far corner of the room she saw a tapered shape and recognized it as Cole's torso. He was lying on the floor, with his back to her.

Relief filtered through her, leaving in its path raw disappointment. Pregnancy hormones must be playing havoc with her mind. She didn't want Cole to sleep in the same bed with her!

Then she remembered his wisecrack about her taking a class on kissing. Had he meant that she didn't know how? Had he not been as affected by their wedding kiss as she had been? Letting out a huff she flipped onto her side. What did she care?

As the minutes ticked into nothingness, she could no longer restrain herself. "What was that supposed to mean?" Her voice sliced through the quiet. "That crack about my taking a class in kissing."

"Nothing."

Irritated more at herself than at Cole, she turned over again, trying to find a comfortable position. She punched her pillow. Their kiss burned in her memory. She wasn't so naive that she didn't know how to kiss. That she couldn't tell when a man was aroused. After all, she was pregnant. She hadn't gotten that way alone.

That only caused more doubts to assail her. Rusty hadn't stuck around for long. Maybe he'd grown bored with her. Maybe she wasn't sexy. Maybe she didn't know how to kiss right.

Irritated more at herself than Cole she sat upright and glared at his corner of the room. "Was it that bad?"

"What?" Cole's voice sounded strained, as if she'd disturbed him from a sound sleep.

Which only made her angrier. How could he sleep when she was only a few feet away? She certainly wasn't going to sleep well tonight with Cole lying on the floor beside her bed wearing—or not wearing—God only knew what.

Her face burned in the darkness. She clutched the sheet in her fisted hands. She expected him to laugh at her, to tell her he'd be willing to give her a few private lessons. "When you kissed me."

"No. You kiss real good." His voice sounded rusty, sexy. Then he coughed softly. "Just remember, you kissed me, too."

The rumbling tone of his voice sent a shimmy of excitement along her skin. Now she wouldn't get a wink of sleep.

Chapter Five

Cole lifted a square bale of hay, which felt like a slab of granite, and carried it to the last stall. He'd never felt so tired in his life. Not even when Haley had been a newborn and he'd bottle-fed her and changed her diapers every three hours during the night. A cranky baby wasn't keeping him up now, though.

Haley hadn't had a nightmare the whole week since Elise had moved in with them. Into *his* room. Where she slept in *his* bed, as soundly as if she'd been anesthetized. He imagined her having sweet dreams. Nothing like what he was suffering only a few measly feet away on the cold, hard floor, wide awake, listening to her soft breathing, waiting for…for what? For her to invite him into what was now *her* bed? That wouldn't happen.

No, he knew what he was waiting for. For Elise to crawl out of bed, pack her suitcase and leave. Okay, he admitted, it didn't make a helluva lot of sense. Why would she leave? She had a nice warm bed, plenty to eat, anything she wanted. But then, so had his ex-wife. He ignored the burning ache in his chest.

Elise was pregnant. Where would she go? He didn't know. It was simply a possibility he wasn't willing to risk. Of course, if she did decide to go he didn't know what he'd do about it. How could he stop her? He couldn't hold her hostage.

As these thoughts swirled around his brain, eventually darkness collapsed upon him and he would dream. Not nightmares, like his daughter had suffered since her mother had left. No, these were hot and erotic and always featured Elise.

Good God, she's pregnant! What was he doing thinking of an expectant mother with tousled hair and kiss-swollen lips? But Elise didn't look pregnant. She didn't act pregnant, either. Weren't expectant mothers supposed to suffer morning sickness?

His first wife had been as cranky as his old tractor starting on a cold morning. To make herself feel better about her burgeoning size, Paula had bought a whole new wardrobe, complete with shoes and accessories. But she'd only complained more afterward.

"Cole?"

He turned as Elise pushed the barn door open wider and peered inside.

"I'm here," he called.

Hesitantly, she entered. She wore a flowing purple skirt that nearly touched her ankles and looked like it had been bound with rubber bands until it came out wrinkled. His gaze settled on her middle which looked almost flat, at least what he could see of it through the elasticized waistband. The blue-jean vest made her breasts seem fuller, and he imagined how they would fit perfectly into the palm of his hand.

"Um, it's so hot out today, I thought you could probably use a break." She held out an ice-filled glass of water.

Surprised by her gesture, he stumbled forward, almost tripping over his own two feet. Paula never would have brought him water, never would have been concerned about the heat or his well-being. "Uh...thanks." He reached for the glass, his fingers grazing hers, sending electric shocks up his arm. "I appreciate it."

"Any time." She glanced down at her feet and then met his gaze squarely. "I want to be a help around here, not a hindrance."

He almost choked on the ice-cold liquid. "You're not. I mean, you are a big help. You help with Haley."

Jerking his attention away from her, he turned back to his task and forked the bale of hay to spread it around the stall. He had to get his libido under control. "Haley make it to school on time?"

"With minutes to spare." She leaned against the gated entrance to the stall. Sunlight glinted off her auburn hair. She wore it loose, and it curled about her shoulders enticingly.

"Thanks for taking her."

"Don't mind a bit. I'm enjoying getting to know her. She's so sweet." She crossed an ankle over her other foot, resting part of her weight on the point of her white tennis shoe and drawing his gaze to her shapely calf. "What are you doing?"

Guilty as charged for imagining things he shouldn't be contemplating, he lifted his gaze to meet hers. What could he say? He was ogling her like she was a model in the *Sports Illustrated*'s swimsuit edition? At least she hadn't made him promise not to *look* at her or *think* about taking her to bed. He just couldn't act on his natural impulse.

"I thought you fed horses hay," she said, glancing at the straw covering the stall floor, "not use it for bedding."

His guilt acted like a sieve as relief poured in that she hadn't caught him staring at her. "It's used for both purposes."

"So what are you doing?"

"Mucking out the stall."

"Mucking? What's that mean?"

His gaze narrowed. "I don't know."

"Why's it called 'mucking'? 'Cause it's such a yucky job?"

Her warm smile caught him by surprise, and he jabbed the pitchfork at a pile of hay. He used too much force and the tongs went straight through and stabbed the hard-packed earth beneath. He jerked the fork back and cursed his stupidity. Why did she affect him this way?

"How often do you do this?" she asked.

Concentrating on his chore, he answered. "Every day."

"That often?"

"Yes." Cole was unable to keep the irritation out of his voice.

"Oh." The corners of her mouth pulled and hurt glimmered in her eyes. "Well, I didn't mean to bother you." She reached for the glass she'd brought.

Damn. Guilt ripped through him. She'd brought water and he'd treated her like an outcast. His irritation wasn't aimed at her, but at himself. He caught her hand, held her when she would have turned away. "I'm sorry, Elise. I didn't mean to snap." He cursed himself for being a fool. And why the hell was he still touching her? He pulled away, wiped his hand on the back of his jeans and grabbed the pitchfork. "I'm just not used to having someone around all the time."

She gave a nod of understanding. "I never realized how much there is to do around a ranch. Can I help?"

This time he missed the pile of hay he'd aimed for and impaled only air, making him stumble forward. He coughed, his ears burning. "You're not dressed for working out here. In this heat."

"Would you let me if I were wearing jeans and boots?"

"Probably not."

"Why?"

"Because." Because he'd have to watch after her, look at her, *try* to ignore her.

"Because I'm a woman?" she asked.

"No." Because she was a sexy woman who he wasn't supposed to want.

She placed a fist on her narrow hip. "Are you sure that's not the reason?"

His frown deepened. "Yes."

"If it's because I'm pregnant, then you don't have to worry. A little work, some exercise, is good for me. That's what the doctor said."

"I'll take care of the ranch. You manage the house."

"It's clean enough to eat off the floors. I'm bored."

A cold draft shot through him, chilling him to the bone. Paula had been bored. Bored enough to abandon her daughter and husband. Would Elise leave? How would that affect Haley? He told himself it wouldn't faze *him*. Not in the least.

"I need to do something." She clasped her hands together as if to keep herself from grabbing the pitchfork out of his hands. "I want to help."

"Why?" he asked, remembering how Paula hadn't wanted anything to do with the horses or cattle, much less dirty her hands by cleaning toilets or dusting furniture.

"I can't just sit around all day counting the seconds. 'm not the type to watch soaps or eat bonbons."

If the image of his first wife hadn't been so clear in his mind and the pain so sharp in his chest, he would have aughed. As pleased as he was that Elise wanted to help, ne still didn't want her underfoot all day. Across the room at night was all his libido could stand. "Why don't you ry your hand at cooking? Would you like to make din- ner?"

"You sure you trust me?"

"Can't be any worse than anything I've cooked for Ha- ley."

She laughed. "I don't know about that. But if you're game, so am I." She took another step into the stall, en- croaching on his space. "But that still doesn't solve the problem of what I'll do until this evening. How about if I organize your tools? I saw that jumble of hardware out on the table."

"Fine." Anything to get a few feet of space. With her so close he couldn't draw a full breath.

With an engaging smile that made him focus on her lips and remember their kiss instead of his chores, she left him alone with his scrambled thoughts. Pushing them from his mind, he concentrated on leading his buckskin mare, Win- nie, back inside the stall. He gave the horse fresh water, feed and a pat on the backside.

Less than an hour later, Elise was back with a plastic bucket full of equipment. "Excuse me, Cole. What's all this?"

He gave her a sidelong glance but continued scooping up manure with the shovel and dumping it in a pail. "Curry combs and brushes for the horses."

"Where do you want them?"

He sighed wearily, more exhausted from fighting his

attraction to her than with answering her questions. "The tack room." Before she could ask the next obvious question he said, "It's next to the entrance."

"Right. Thanks." She darted out of the stall but appeared a few minutes later. "Now what?"

"You finished all that?"

She held up her grease and dirt-streaked hands. "You are now as organized as a library."

"Will I be able to find anything?"

"Not a problem. If you can't find something, just ask me."

Great. What if she wasn't around? What if she left? Again, that fear resurfaced and made his shoulder blades pinch together.

"So now what can I do?" The eagerness in her eyes caught him off guard.

What was it about Elise that got to him? Her enthusiasm, her willingness, her sweet spirit unnerved him. He'd never known anyone like her—so willing to help, so determined to make a better life for her own child. Paula never would have married for the sake of her child. In that regard he definitely could relate to Elise. He understood her parental role, probably better than she did herself.

If only she'd remind him of his ex-wife, then he'd be able to ignore her. But Elise wasn't anything like Paula. That should have assuaged his fears about her leaving. Instead, he worried that he cared too much. And he'd sworn to himself that he'd never love again.

This, too, shall pass, Elise figured as she grabbed two eggs out of the refrigerator.

The awkwardness between Cole and her would fade with time. It had to be difficult for him to suddenly have strange woman puttering around his house, folding his underwear and kicking him out of his own bed.

Her own nervousness was understandable, especially with him sleeping in the same room, only a few feet away. Guilt wrenched her insides into knots. For a week she'd watched him collapse with exhaustion onto his makeshift bed on the floor. She'd contemplated inviting him to share the bed with her, but then she'd worried he'd take that as a different kind of invitation. In the end, she'd rolled over and gone to sleep.

With time, she hoped, her nerves would untangle and the doubts would fade into the distance. Still, she wondered if she could fit into Cole's family. Could she hold up her end of the bargain? Or would he dump her the way Rusty had?

She needed—longed for—some kind of security. She'd believed a marriage license would provide that. But it hadn't. Cole's cool detachment kept her off balance, and she wondered constantly if he regretted marrying her. More than anything she wanted to prove she could be a good wife and mother. But how?

The answers eluded her. So she vacuumed, dusted and played taxi driver for Haley. Elise didn't know how to treat a husband or even how to fix a casserole. Why then had she volunteered to cook dinner tonight? She'd make a mess of things for sure.

Angling an egg over the side of the mixing bowl she cracked it against the side. The shell collapsed in her hand, the gooey egg white oozed out and coated her fingers. The yolk slipped into the bowl along with pieces of the shell. Elise grimaced as she imagined Cole biting into the meat loaf and getting eggshell between his teeth.

As she picked out the tiny pieces, she prayed her attraction to Cole would cool. Every time she watched him work, sweat beading his brow and glistening on his skin, she tingled all over, as if she had a fever. When he held his daughter close and gave her one of his dazzling, dimpled smiles, her heart melted. With each touch, whether it was a hand grazing her arm or a gentle kiss on the cheek in front of Haley, her thoughts steamed up faster than car windows with a teenage couple inside.

She *had* to control her responses to Cole. She simply wouldn't think about the kiss he'd given her at their wedding anymore. She certainly wouldn't think about the way one hooded glance from him could give her goose bumps and a hot flash at the same time.

"How's it coming?" Cole asked, as he walked through the back door and placed his Stetson on a wooden peg. Dirt caked his boots and spotted his chambray shirt.

At least he'd gone back to wearing a shirt, Elise thought, remembering his sun-bronzed skin gleaming that first day she'd driven to the ranch to apply to be his mail-order bride. A heated flurry stirred in her belly. Pushing aside her reaction to him, she reached for the package of ground beef. "Dinner should be ready in an hour."

He stopped beside her, and she breathed in the scent of Cole mingled with the outdoor aromas of cedar and leather. Her insides twisted into knots. Leaning over her shoulder, much too close for comfort, he asked, "What are we having?"

"Meat loaf," she answered, her voice tight.

"Hmm." The slow rumble in his chest rattled her composure. "My favorite."

Elise breathed a sigh of relief. MaryAnn had been right. She'd mentioned the fact the night of their wedding while they'd fried catfish.

"How does he like it?" Elise had asked MaryAnn, hoping for a recipe she could borrow without giving away that she was lost in a kitchen.

"Oh, just normal ol' meatloaf," MaryAnn had answered, shrugging. "I think his momma used regular soda crackers. Nothing fancy. But I think he likes barbecue sauce instead of ketchup. I'm sure however you fix it will be just fine. A man in love don't care a whit about how a woman cooks. It's after the honeymoon phase that a man starts to feel a different kind of hunger." She gave a wink that set Elise's nerves on edge.

Trouble was, Cole wasn't in love. There wasn't a honeymoon to distract him. And there wouldn't be. So her cooking skills—or lack of—mattered.

Crackers? Ketchup? What else went into meat loaf? She'd searched the kitchen all afternoon for a recipe but hadn't found one, so she was winging it. What was meat loaf anyway? A hodgepodge of ingredients. Who would know the difference?

Cole edged past her, placing a hand against her waist. His chest brushed her back. The kitchen wasn't small, but it seemed to shrink when he entered the room. "I'll be back after a shower." He left her alone with her simmering thoughts. On his way through the den he called, "Haley, set the table for dinner."

"Yes, sir," the little girl answered.

A minute later Elise heard the rubber soles of Haley's tennis shoes tapping the hardwood floors. "Can I squish it?"

"Excuse me?" Elise asked, confused.

"Daddy always lets me squeeze all the stuff together."

"Oh. Well, okay. Wash your hands first." She pulled a chair up to the counter and helped Haley climb onto it.

"I like to cook, don't you?" The little girl's pigtails bobbed with her enthusiasm.

"I...I..." She'd never made the effort. Or had the desire. Or the chance. Growing up in the orphanage, the meals had always been prepared by others. After she'd left and been on her own, she'd never taken the time to learn how to do much of anything in a kitchen besides fix sandwiches. Now she wanted to miraculously turn herself into Martha Stewart. "I like cooking with you."

Haley grinned, and her cheeks dimpled. "Me, too."

"What's your favorite thing to cook?" Elise asked, putting the mixing bowl in front of the little girl.

"Chocolate chip cookies."

"Mmm. We'll have to make a batch then."

Haley gave Elise a sidelong glance. "I like to eat the dough."

Elise ruffled the little girl's hair and smiled. "Me, too."

Haley pushed her long sleeves above her elbows. One slid back down her arm and Elise took the end and rolled it up. "What do you like to make?"

"I don't really know. See, I never had the opportunity to cook when I was a girl."

Haley cocked her head to the side. "How come?"

Elise's insides shifted restlessly. How should she answer? She rarely spoke of her childhood. She'd tried to forget the loneliness, disappointments and pain, but she couldn't. "I lived in an orphanage. I didn't have a mommy or daddy to show me how."

"Did that make you sad?"

Elise picked a piece of lint off a dish towel. "Sometimes."

"I used to get sad, too," Haley said matter-of-factly. "'Cause Momma left us. But I prayed real hard that we'd get a new mommy who'd love us. And God sent you."

Tears burned the backs of Elise's eyes. She blinked and swallowed hard. She'd given up praying for a family a long time ago. But maybe God had finally heard the prayers of a lonely little girl. She prayed silently He wouldn't take this away.

Haley reached around Elise and gave her a strangling hug. "You don't have to be sad no more."

Sniffing back the emotions that threatened to bring her to her knees, Elise patted the little girl on the back. "Better get busy mixing that stuff together or dinner will never be ready."

Haley plunged her hands into the gooey mess, squeezing the ground beef between her fingers. "Are you gonna add onions? Daddy always puts onions in meat loaf."

"Onions? Of course!" Why hadn't she thought of that? What else had she left out? Elise turned back toward the refrigerator. Why hadn't she thought to ask his daughter? "How much does your daddy usually put in?"

"Oh, a lot." Haley flexed her fingers in the mixture and nodding knowingly. "He loves onions. Momma didn't like 'em though. She said they stunk."

Elise wondered about Cole's ex-wife but she wouldn't ask Haley. Maybe someday Cole would trust her enough to explain what had happened with his first marriage. She found the chopping block and began cutting the onion into tiny bits. The pungent odor tingled her nose and stung her eyes. "Can you think of anything else I forgot to add?"

Haley squinched up her freckled features. "Don't know what it's called. It's this red stuff."

"Red?" Elise glanced around the kitchen.

"It's like water."

"Red water?" Elise lifted one eyebrow skeptically. "You mean Kool-Aid?"

"Nah. I'll show you."

After the meat concoction came out of the oven, the vegetables placed on the table and the drinks poured, Haley called her father to dinner. They sat at the table in their newly designated places with Cole at the head and his daughter across from Elise.

"Can I say the prayer?" Haley slid one of her feet under her bottom and grasped both of her parents' hands.

"Of course, darlin'. Go ahead." Cole held out his hand for Elise to take.

She paused. Their gazes met. A flush of heat rose inside her. Since she'd learned this ritual on their wedding night, she'd both dreaded and anticipated the touch of his warm, calloused hand each night. His fingers entwined with hers, and awareness rippled down her spine making her toes curl under.

"Dear God, thank you for my new mommy." The girl's tiny voice struck a raw nerve in Elise. She felt Cole's hand tighten on hers. "Help her to like us. Amen."

Elise felt her chest compress with emotions she'd never owned, never been given. This little girl's love and acceptance was a gift she didn't take lightly. It somehow made the situation of living in a loveless marriage easier.

Haley glanced up and then giggled. "Oops. And thanks for this food."

Cole cleared his throat and released Elise's hand. She glanced from father to daughter, her heart swelling with happiness. This was her family now. She touched the slight roundness of her stomach. It would be her baby's family, too. Maybe this was the security she'd been searching for after all.

"How much meat loaf do you want?" Cole asked, angling the knife over the rounded lump of meat.

Elise's heart pounded. This was the first meal she'd cooked, the first of many for *her* new family. She wanted it to be perfect. She'd even put sprigs of parsley around the platter to make it look like something from one of those cooking shows.

"Lots, Daddy, I'm hungry." Haley handed him her plate.

He sliced into the loaf and it crumbled into pieces.

"Oh, no," Elise cried, her heart tumbling over.

"Doesn't matter what it looks like," Cole said, scooping up the meat with a serving spoon. "It's the taste that matters."

"That's right," Haley added. "It all looks the same anyways when it gets chewed up and swallowed."

Elise twisted her hands together as her nerves tightened around her spine. "I hope it tastes okay. I didn't have a recipe."

Cole sent her an understanding wink that made her stomach free-fall. "There aren't recipes for meat loaf. You can add anything you want." His brow creased, and he gave her a sidelong glance. He studied the meat loaf more closely and took a whiff of the spicy aroma. "What did you put in it?"

"Worried?" she asked.

"Just want to be sure we can duplicate it. Right, Haley?"

"Uh-huh." His daughter grabbed her fork and dug into the mixture. "But I can tell you. 'Cause I helped."

"She sure did." Elise smiled at her. "She's a good helper. She knew where everything in the kitchen was."

Haley beamed. "We put all your favorite stuff in it."

"I bet it'll be great then." Cole took a big bite.

Elise watched him, hoping he'd be pleased at her attempt. He chewed enthusiastically then slowed his pace. His eyes bulged, and then watered. Before he could holler for help, Elise handed him his glass of water as her heart caved in on itself. He gulped down his drink.

"Good, huh, Daddy?"

He nodded, unable to speak.

Elise dipped her chin, trying to hide her disappointment. Cole placed a hand on her arm. Anxious, she lifted her gaze. "Too much Tabasco sauce?"

"Perfect," he rasped. "Right amount of onions, too." Then he downed Elise's glass of water.

Elise blinked back tears. Her throat burned. Her stomach tightened. "Excuse me," she said, pushing away from the table. "I forgot…something…"

She raced into the den, gulping in air like she was suffocating. She'd failed. Cole had given her so much—a home, a family. What had she given him? Probably more headaches. And she couldn't even make a meat loaf!

"What's the matter with Elise, Daddy?" Haley asked, her brown eyes focused on the closed door leading to the den.

"Nothing, darlin'." He shoved back his chair and stood. "I'll be right back. Go ahead and eat." He headed toward the den, stopped, and turned back to his daughter. "Um…why don't you make yourself a peanut butter and jelly sandwich?"

"Didn't you like the meatloaf?"

"Sure I did, sweetheart, but it's too…spicy for you."

He walked into the den, but found it empty. Winding his way up the stairs he entered his—their—bedroom without knocking. Elise sat on the side of the bed, her hands clasped tightly in her lap, her head bowed.

"Are you okay?" he asked.

She nodded and sniffed.

"It wasn't that bad. Honest."

"You don't have to be nice to me."

He moved toward her and eased down onto the bed beside her. He started to put his arm around her, but remembered where they were—and his promise—and thought better of it. "Look, so it wasn't great. I didn't marry you because you're a sensational cook. Frankly, I'm not much better. Just takes a little practice, is all."

She looked up, and her eyes were red-rimmed from tears. Her cheeks were damp. "Why did you marry me? I mean, I know you wanted a mail-order bride, one you didn't have to romance. But why me? I think you could have found somebody better."

"I don't," he said with conviction. "I wanted someone to mother my daughter—"

"How can I be a wife or a mother if I can't cook?" The strain in her voice tugged at him.

"You didn't let me finish. You're great with Haley. She loves you already. Lots of great mothers can't cook. It's no big deal. That can be learned. But mothering can't. You're either good at it or you're not. And you, Elise, are the best."

"I am?"

He touched her then, pressed his hand against the side of her face, cupping her jawline. His thumb wiped away a tear at the corner of her mouth. An electrical current ripped up his arm and zapped his heart.

"I don't want you to regret marrying me, Cole."

Regret? His only regret was that he'd agreed not to make love with her. Granted, he'd rather have his wife in his bed, or rather to be in bed with her, but he felt proud he'd made the right decision in marrying her. "I don't."

And he knew at that moment that he already cared too much about Elise.

"Do you miss working at Chuck's Diner?" Cole wasn't sure what had spurred him to ask the question. Maybe it was her comment a week earlier about being bored that still haunted him.

Elise glanced up from the kitchen table and stuck Haley's number-two pencil behind her ear. "Hmm, do I miss waiting on grouchy ranchers? Getting measly tips that never add up to cover the rent? Scrubbing Jell-O and scrambled eggs off the linoleum?" Her brow wrinkled with contemplation. "Gosh, that's a tough one. Nope. Can't say that I do."

"You like being here with us, don't you?" Haley said grinning.

"Of course I do. I'd much rather clean up your spills than Chuck's or Orie Simpson's."

"Ooh! He's gross." Haley scrunched up her features. "He gets in trouble all the time at school. Yesterday he sucked Jell-O up his nose."

Elise laughed. The light tinkling sound coiled Cole's nerves into a tight ball of confusion. How could he be wary of her and so attracted to her at the same time?

One day he'd found her trying to reach the top shelf of the pantry. Foolishly, he'd walked up behind her and grabbed the tomato-soup can for her. She'd jumped in surprise and her backside brushed against him in a very intimate way.

He'd learned over the past two weeks of marriage that Elise didn't like to be idle. As the days dominoed, he'd watched her rearrange closets, help muck out the stalls and plant marigolds in window boxes. He'd come to admire and respect her determination, drive and spirit. And he'd learned to avoid getting so close to her.

"Better go get ready for bed, Haley," he said, noticing the time on the mantel clock.

"Oh, Daddy!" His daughter began the nightly ritual of sticking out her bottom lip.

"It's that time," Elise said. "Tell you what. I'll be upstairs in five minutes to tuck you in and read you a story."

"You, too, Daddy?"

"Wouldn't miss it for the world."

"I'll hurry then." Haley hugged Elise who gave her an affectionate squeeze.

Cole watched the two, his heart swelling. He had definitely made the right decision. No matter how difficult it was for him to be married and yet not truly *married*.

"Don't forget to brush your teeth," Cole called after his daughter who bounded up the stairs.

Elise chuckled and stacked his daughter's school supplies on the table. "Why'd you ask if I missed working at Chuck's?"

Cole ran his hands down the crease in his jeans. How could he explain his concern that she'd get bored like Paula had? "I don't know. Maybe I thought you were working too hard." He noticed then that she had dark smudges under her eyes. "You look tired."

"I am." She yawned and stretched. Her breasts pushed against her cotton blouse, tempting him to forget the promise he'd made. "It's been a long day. I got sleepy this afternoon. But that's normal for a pregnancy."

"It is?"

"Oh, sure. Makes you want to sleep all the time." She smiled, and an inner glow lit up her hazel eyes like sequins glimmering in the light. "But I've been pretty lucky. I've only been queasy a few times, and only when I hadn't eaten in a while, but I've never had real morning sickness."

"Haley's mother had a rough time of it."

"Oh?" Elise sat on the couch across from him. "Was she horribly sick?"

No, just horrible. "She didn't like being pregnant. Wouldn't have mattered if she was sick or not."

Elise clasped her hands together. "I can't imagine feeling that way. But I've heard stories that make me wonder why so many women have more than one baby." She smiled. "Why do folks have to tell you the worst experiences they've ever heard as soon as they learn you're pregnant?"

He laughed. "I don't know." He decided to keep his own horror stories to himself. "Tell you what—I'll make you a promise that I won't do that."

She nodded, but her brow creased. "When do you think we should tell Haley about the baby?"

He thrust his fingers through his hair. "I've been thinking about that, trying to figure it out." His gaze shifted to her waist. "You're not really showing yet."

She straightened, pushing her breasts against her soft, cotton top and making his gut contract. She splayed her fingers across her abdomen. "You don't think so? I've been feeling huge. Maybe I've been just looking for an excuse to go buy some maternity clothes."

His spine stiffened. How often had he heard his ex-wife complain about not having a shopping mall nearby? She'd longed for the big city, any city bigger than Desert Springs, for a reason to get off the ranch even for a few hours. "Eager to get to Amarillo?"

"Oh, I'm sure whatever I need I can find in Desert Springs. But I'm just anxious to look pregnant."

Surprised, he said, "Then we better tell Haley soon."

"And everyone else." Her knowing look reminded him others would quickly realize Elise got pregnant before they married. He hoped the scandal wouldn't be too severe. Already he'd been asked by Chuck if his new wife was all right, since she'd been to the doctor's a few times. Wouldn't take long for the rumor mills to start churning.

"Why don't we wait a couple more weeks?" he suggested, wanting to postpone the inevitable. He wasn't sure how Haley would take the news. She'd asked for a mommy, not a baby brother or sister. She might feel threatened. She might resent the upheaval. Guilt saturated his soul. Had he made the wrong decision in getting married? In marrying Elise?

His gut instinct told him no. Even though his heart floundered with doubt and fear.

"If that's what you want, we'll wait." The dark splotches under her eyes gave her a haunted look.

"I'm ready!" His daughter's voice brought him to his feet.

"Let's go tuck her in."

"Then I'm turning in," Elise said. "I'm bushed."

He stifled a groan. He'd suffer another sleepless night with her across the room. So close and yet so far.

Chapter Six

"Daddy!"

Haley's cry yanked Cole out of a restless sleep. With his heart pounding, he rolled over on his hard pallet just as the bedroom door opened.

"Haley?" He leapt to his feet. "Are you okay?"

"What's wrong?" Elise asked almost simultaneously as she sat up in bed.

Haley stood in the doorway, her nightgown brushing her toes, her hair mussed from sleep, her fist rubbing her eyes. "I had a bad dream."

Cole blinked away the last bit of sleep and realized his daughter was okay, only scared. Just another bad dream. But it wasn't a fever or anything else. He took a step toward his daughter and froze.

We're caught! What would his daughter say about him sleeping on the floor? Would she think this was normal behavior between married couples? Would she ask? Would she tell her classmates or her teacher? Cole's head began to throb.

Without pausing, Elise flung back her covers and reached for Haley. She embraced his daughter and pulled her onto the edge of the bed. "Everything's all right now."

"I dreamed you left us," Haley whined, her little arms clutching Elise.

Cole had experienced the same dream in the past weeks. It made no sense. Elise seemed content. She seemed to like them, the ranch, her new life. But still the unreasonable fear haunted him.

"Oh, sweetheart," Elise cooed, "I'm here. Right here. Do you want to sleep with me?…uh…" Her gaze collided with Cole's, panic making her eyes round. "I mean, with your daddy and me?"

Haley snuffled and nodded.

Elise shifted, settling Haley into the middle of the bed. She gave Cole a steady look. "It's okay," she whispered against the top of Haley's blond curls, but she spoke pointedly to him. Her gaze shifted to the empty space in the bed, a space she'd left for Cole. "Let's all go to sleep."

Reluctantly, knowing this was a mistake but at the same time his only choice, Cole climbed into his side of the bed and wondered how he'd ever sleep with Elise so close, yet so far away.

Cole stared into the darkness, his heart thudding impatiently in his chest. He could hear Elise's soft breathing and knew she was sound asleep. Next to him. Only a few inches away. More than anything, he wanted to stir Elise awake with soft, slow kisses. But he'd made a damn promise.

"No more sleeping on the floor," Elise had said one week ago, the day after Haley's nightmare. "We can't take a chance. If Haley is going to believe this marriage is real, and if she might barge in on us in the middle of the night, then you need to be in your own bed. Not on the floor.''

"But," he'd argued, his pulse galloping, "she didn't notice."

"This time."

"I could put a lock on the door," he'd suggested, his mind conjuring up too many images of Elise, images he couldn't erase and couldn't ignore, images that made him want to make love to her.

"And lock out your daughter?"

With a heavy sigh of resignation, he knew she was right. He just hadn't known how he'd live with sleeping—only sleeping—with Elise in the same bed!

"Don't worry," she said with a soft smile that had curled his insides into knots, "I trust you not to break your promise."

How would he survive more of this slow, methodical torture?

Elise drifted on a soft cloud. She was warm. She was safe, safer than she'd ever been, ever imagined possible. She snuggled deeper beneath the covers and felt a velvety texture tickle her cheek. She breathed deeply, inhaling an intoxicating scent that was pure, raw male.

Ah, this was some dream. A dream she'd had often since her teens. Her Prince Charming had arrived. She embraced the dream and her handsome prince, wrapping her arms around his lean, bare torso. She felt his hands drift over her, exploring her back, grazing the sides of her breasts, molding her against his body. He planted tiny kisses across her brow, and she lifted her face for that fairy-tale kiss that she knew would follow.

His lips were warm, insistent and she opened to him. For she knew when she opened her eyes he would vanish, as he had all the years before. But in her dreams, he existed and lived and belonged only to her.

"Oh, Elise," his voice sounded husky, sexy and suddenly familiar.

Her eyes opened. "Cole!"

He met her accusatory stare with a sleepy but hungry look. "What?" Then he blinked. "Oh." He pushed away from her before she could and rolled out of bed. "Damn."

She clutched the blanket to her chest and struggled to a sitting position, her body weakened by his potent kiss. "I—I...uh..."

"I'm sorry," he said. "That was a mistake." He grabbed his jeans and yanked them on. The muscles along his chest contracted and flexed with each rough movement. "Hell, Elise, I know I made you a promise. But... damn..." He shoved his fingers through his hair. "It won't happen again."

He strode out of the room, and she knew instinctively where he was headed—the barn. She fell back against the headboard and exhaled slowly even though her heart beat frantically. Could Cole be her Prince Charming?

Cabin fever. That was his problem, even though it was a hundred degrees outside. Feeling trapped, he decided, wasn't simply a malady of a wintry climate. Maybe the blaze of a summer heat wave made it worse. Or Elise did.

There was only one solution.

He pushed open the barn door and strode toward the house. Since his marriage to her he'd been distracted, almost crazed, with an insatiable need that only Elise could quench. Now he had focus. With each step his purpose grew more intense. He shut the front door behind him, louder than he'd intended, and the sound ricocheted through the house.

Elise poked her head around the corner from the kitchen. She held a spatula in one hand and an oven mitt in the other. The sweet aroma of warm chocolate wafted through the house. "Something wrong?"

Cole frowned. "Yes. No." He spit out a curse word. "I mean…"

Elise tilted her head to the side, studying him. A worry line drew her eyebrows together.

He shoved his fingers through his hair. How the hell was he supposed to explain it? He couldn't breathe here anymore. He needed to get away. From *her!* Before he made a fool of himself. Before he broke his promise and forced himself on her. Before he went loco.

Her arm fell to her side, and she took a step forward. "What is it?" she asked, her voice whisper soft. Her eyes were wide with worry—no, he reevaluated—fear. Her fingers clenching the spatula turned white. "Is Haley all right?"

He nodded. "She's swinging on the porch."

"Then what?" She paled. "Did I do something?"

"No." *Yes!* Not really. Not enough. That was the problem. It wasn't her, so much as it was him. Damn him for being a fool, for wanting her so much.

He swung around and started pacing. He felt caged in, unable to escape the yearnings, longings and needs that burned like a raging fire when he was near her, when he could smell her light, airy fragrance, when he looked into those warm-hearted hazel eyes. He couldn't tell her what was going on inside him. Hell, he wasn't sure himself. It made no sense. He had to get control of himself.

Finally, he said, "I'm going to town tonight."

"Oh?"

"I—I… It's something I have to do."

"Can I help?" Her constant eagerness to assist gnawed at him, chewed through his selfishness.

He swallowed the guilt and the urge to tell her exactly what she could do to "help" him. "No. I'm okay."

"Will you be here for dinner?" she asked, her voice controlled but concern underlined each word.

He shook his head.

Silence ticked loudly in the room. He glanced away from her probing stare. There wasn't anything wrong with needing to get away, with wanting some time alone. How many married men enjoyed a "boys' night out"? It wasn't as if he was going out on the town, looking to pick up women. Not when the woman he wanted was under his very own roof.

The oven's buzzer sounded but the ringing continued in his head long after she'd turned off the timer. He heard the squeak of the oven door and the rattle of a pan. Following after her when he should have retreated, he watched her pull out a tray of golden-brown chocolate chip cookies.

"Haley's favorite," he stated, still stunned by the revelation that he wanted Elise. No other woman would do.

She nodded. "That's what she told me. I thought I'd send them to school with her on Monday. Since it's the last week before summer break."

That's why he wanted her. Yes, she was beautiful. But it was the little things she did that endeared her to him. That's what was so dangerous about her.

Moved that Elise had taken the effort to please his daughter, he felt another helping of guilt being heaped on top of him. Why was he so selfish, when Elise was bending over backwards to meet her end of their bargain? What had gotten into him? This was *his* problem, not theirs and certainly not hers. There was no need to punish Elise or Haley.

"We'll be fine tonight alone," Elise said, putting another tray of cookies into the oven. "So don't worry."

He cursed himself for being an idiot. He didn't want to go off by himself. Yes, he wanted to keep his distance from Elise. But he also enjoyed her company. He'd trapped himself.

"We're all going," he proclaimed correcting his earlier statement. Maybe he simply needed a change of scenery, one that wasn't as cozy or intimate as his house and bedroom.

She blinked. "We? But I thought you said you were going."

"I changed my mind." And heart.

"Are we going out for dinner?" A spark of excitement and adventure brightened her eyes and ignited a fire inside him.

That's all he needed—a nice, quiet romantic dinner with Elise. No way! He grabbed the first safe thought that came to him. "It's bingo night at the church."

Bingo? Cole didn't strike Elise as a bingo player. Poker, maybe. She never could tell what he was thinking; he held his thoughts as carefully and cautiously as a hand of cards.

"Aren't you feeling well?" Cole asked that evening as they piled into his pickup. He'd dressed in his usual jeans and starched, button-down shirt. His boots were shined to a spit-polish, and, with his Stetson shading his eyes, he looked as sexy as James Dean.

Haley sat between them. Nervous energy racing through Elise's veins, she clenched and unclenched her hands. She felt like a mannequin on display in a store window. Had she worn the right outfit? What did one wear to play bingo on Saturday night? In her case, whatever clothes fit.

"I'm fine," she said, her voice strained.

"You sure?" Cole turned the ignition and shifted into reverse. "You look tired."

Great. She'd tried to look her best, to hide the blue smudges beneath her eyes. She wanted to please him, make him proud. Pressing her fingers against a wrinkle in her cotton skirt, she wished she could wear a pair of tight-fitting jeans or maybe a sexy mini-skirt. But this full skirt was all she had that still fit around her expanding waist. "I'm okay."

She reminded herself of that fact over and over in her head. She was okay. She'd be okay. She didn't need love. More specifically, she didn't need Cole's love. She had a roof over her head, food to eat and the semblance of a family. What more did she need?

"Nervous?" he asked, his gaze studying her over the top of Haley's head before he put his foot on the gas.

"A little," she confessed, touched that he'd understood.

"How come?" Haley asked.

"I don't know anyone," Elise answered, trying to simplify the complex emotions fermenting inside her.

Haley put her hand on Elise's. "Don't worry. I'll be there. You can talk to me and Daddy." Her smile widened. "And you know Aunt MaryAnn and Uncle Jack."

Cole nodded. "They'll probably be there." He shot Elise a quick grin that sent a ripple of awareness through her stomach. "It'll be okay. Everyone will like you."

"You don't think they'll be mad?" she asked, twisting her purse strings around her fingers.

He kept his gaze on the highway, but a crease furrowed his brow. "Who?"

"All the women."

He laughed, a hearty robust laugh that popped the tension in her like a pin poking a balloon. "Whatever for?"

She shrugged, embarrassed that she'd mentioned this concern. "Because I stole a very eligible bachelor. I bet there are women who had their eye on you. If not for themselves then for a single daughter or niece."

Still chuckling, he shook his head. "I doubt that. I'm not that great of a catch."

She knew better. He was ruggedly handsome, considerate and a loving father. And he made her skin tingle when he touched her. What more could a woman want?

Her heart contracted. She knew the answer—love. But she didn't want to face that reality.

"Are y'all hungry?" he asked, changing the subject.

She shook her head no. She didn't think she could push anything past the lump in her throat or the knot in her stomach.

"I am!" Haley wiggled in her seat, but the seat belt kept her securely in place. "There's popcorn, hot dogs and nachos at church." Her voice buoyed with excitement. "Sometimes Daddy lets me get a bag of candy." She slanted her gaze toward her father as if hinting that she'd like that kind of a treat tonight. "Can I get a soda, Daddy?"

"Sure, baby. Anything you want."

Too bad Elise couldn't have anything she wanted. Because what she wanted was as elusive and distant as a dream.

They walked into the reception hall at the church, all three of them holding hands, Haley acting as the bridge between Cole and Elise. The greasy odor of hot dogs and spicy scent of jalapeños greeted Elise and made her stomach begin to churn.

The grand hall was as plain as a paper bag but large enough for a wedding reception. Elise blocked those thoughts. She'd had the only wedding and reception she'd ever have—a justice of the peace's ceremony and fish fry—every girl's dream.

A bingo game was already in progress with the caller announcing "B-nine" over the crackling PA system. The families already gathered were scattered among the dozen rectangular tables set up two-by-two down the middle of the room.

"Look, here are the newlyweds!" someone from Elise's left called.

All eyes turned toward them, focusing on Elise, evaluating her. Her nerves buckled. How many times had she been appraised in the past and been found lacking? And why did it matter so much now?

Cole gave her a wink that didn't soothe her nerves at all, but only jumbled her thoughts even more. In defense, as she'd always done, she lifted her chin defiantly, not caring what the others thought about her, and she followed her new husband and daughter into the hall.

Cole gave a brief nod of acknowledgment to neighbors and friends, murmuring a hello to a scant few, offering a wave to others. Smiles blossomed around the room like bluebonnets in spring. He led his family to a yellow-checked table near the front of the room. "I'll pick us up some bingo cards and be right back."

Feeling awkward as a sitting duck, Elise said, "Why don't I go with Haley to get us all some refreshments?"

"Great." Cole reached into his pocket and retrieved his wallet. "This ought to cover it."

"What would you like?" Elise asked.

He removed his sunglasses and his hooded gaze met hers, sending a sizzling sensation straight through her. She sensed he was about to say he wanted her, remembered their kiss, but that was as ridiculous as a girl like her meeting her Prince Charming. "A soda and a couple of hot dogs."

"Come on." Haley took the money from her daddy and tugged on Elise's hand. "I want nachos. What are you gonna have?"

Following the little girl, Elise forced herself to quit staring at Cole. Slowly she shifted her gaze and caught herself before she tripped over a chair. "You'll have to help me decide."

Along one wall was a large window opening that looked into the kitchen area. A line had formed, and several women bustled about the cramped kitchen, popping corn, grilling hot dogs and pouring a cheese sauce over tortilla chips. Together, Haley and Elise took their place at the back of the line.

A gray-haired woman who reminded Elise of an overweight Alice on *The Brady Bunch* stood in front of them. Turning, she said, "So, you're the one that snagged Cole Dalton. Didn't think anyone would waltz him down the aisle...not after..." She waved her hands as if brushing away the past and smiled. "Well, anyway, congratulations, my dear."

"Thank you." *I think.* Confused, Elise stuck out her hand and said, "I'm Elise."

"Nice to know you." The woman shook her hand. "I'm Tiny Ramsey. My given name is Tina Marie Bartles, but everybody calls me Tiny, have since I was knee-high to a tadpole."

Elise wasn't sure why, seeing that the woman outweighed most of the men at the church by a good forty pounds.

Nodding toward the far side of the room, Tiny added,

"I'm married to that hunk of man who's talking to your husband over there."

Elise's gaze shifted to a tall, lanky, white-haired man, and then she focused on Cole. It amazed her that even from this distance his handsome face, broad shoulders, and rugged body could make her stomach tighten. Maybe it was the baby. Maybe she was having "evening" sickness. Or Cole sickness. He caught her staring at him and sent her a smile that frizzed the hair at her nape.

"I'm pleased as punch that Cole found somebody who could make him happy. And you obviously have," Tiny said, fanning herself with a bingo card. "Lordy, the way he looks at you. My, my, makes my heart flutter just thinking about it."

Heat inched its way from Elise's toes to her hairline. Did Cole smile at her differently from how he smiled at other women? Elise doubted that. Shoving away her disappointment, she asked, "Have you lived here long?"

"All my life. I grew up in town, but when I married Eli we settled in the country. Our place isn't too far from yours. You and Cole will have to come over for dinner real soon." Tiny bent down and tugged on Haley's pigtail. "And you, too, sugar. How are you liking having a new momma?"

Haley grinned. "We got our happily ever after now."

The words cut through Elise's heart. She might have a happy ending herself if she weren't afraid Cole would reject her.

"Way to go, Dalton," Eli Ramsey said, sucking on his cigar. "You got a looker there."

"Thanks." Cole glanced over his shoulder and saw Elise holding his daughter's hand. His throat tightened as well as another part of his anatomy. He didn't need to be reminded of his wife's beauty. He needed to get her out of his head, out of his dreams, out of his heart.

Whoa! He wasn't in love with Elise. No, sir. He wouldn't allow himself to fall in love again. Sure, he liked her. Liked her a lot. Appreciated all she did for both Haley and him. And she was pretty. Prettier than he deserved. He was simply grateful to her. She was turning out to be a terrific mother for his daughter. Isn't that what he wanted?

Of course. But part of him wanted more. What his great-great-grandfather had.

"Wasn't she waitressing for a while over at Chuck's?" Eli asked, studying his cigar and then rolling it between his fingers.

Cole nodded and picked up three bingo boards for his family. *His* family. It had a nice ring to it.

For a moment he flashed back to another time, another marriage. He'd wanted to be a family, but it had never worked out that way. He'd wanted to go places with Paula when Haley was a baby, but his ex-wife had scoffed at the "trivial, boring and stupid" activities in town. She hadn't just wanted off the ranch. She'd wanted out of Desert Springs.

But Cole loved his hometown, the people, the sense of community. He liked the fact that when Eli had been stricken with a heart attack, the townsfolk had chipped in to help pay what his insurance hadn't covered. It made him proud that the ranchers in the area had taken turns helping to bale Eli's hay that summer. Since Cole's divorce from Paula, the women in town had taken Haley under their mother-hen wings and loved her like one of their own little chicks.

Maybe that's why he'd asked Elise to come tonight. It was a test to see if she'd have the same reaction Paula had.

Or maybe he'd simply wanted to be with her, wanted an excuse to treat her like his wife. That thought unraveled his nerves.

"Oh, Lord," Eli grunted, "no tellin' what that wife of mine is up to. If y'all weren't already married I'd guess she was matchmakin'." He shook his head. "You bring your new wife over for dinner real soon, all right, Dalton?"

"Will do."

He felt reassured that Tiny Ramsey, the school librarian, would make Elise feel as welcome as apple pie.

"You keep an eye on that bride of yours." Eli clapped Cole on the shoulder. "Wouldn't want one of these fellows to snatch her away from you. She's some catch."

That she was. Cole felt a surge of pride that the men envied him his choice of a bride. "I'm not going to let Elise get away."

Not this time. Not ever.

But, damn, the only way to keep her was not to love her. And that was becoming harder to do.

Cole turned and bumped into Jack.

"How's it going, mister bridegroom?" The lanky rancher gave him a broad wink. "Ready for us to babysit Haley for a night or two, so you and the missus can have some time to yourselves?"

The tips of Cole's ears burned. "Ah, we're doing just fine at the moment. I think Haley needs to be with us for a while longer before we worry about an official…"

"Honeymoon?" Jack finished the sentence for him.

Cole nodded. The idea made his insides tighten with desire. What he wouldn't give to go on a weekend trip with Elise, to be alone with her, to make love with her. But that wouldn't happen. At least not for a while. After her baby arrived, he'd change her mind. Somehow.

"How come you're all the way over here and your bride is standing over there talking to Tiny and MaryAnn?" Jack asked, teasing Cole. "Trouble in paradise already?"

Cole frowned. "Can't get away from so many nosy neighbors."

Jack laughed. "Don't forget my offer."

"I won't." How could he? All he could think about day—and especially night—was making love to his wife.

"Bingo!" Haley bounced out of her chair and almost tipped it over. "Look, Daddy, Elise! I got a bingo!"

Smiling, Elise gave the girl a congratulatory hug, and Haley's arms wrapped around her neck, squeezing with enthusiasm. It made Elise count her blessings, what she had now—which was more than she'd ever had—rather than what would never be. Her gaze met Cole's over the little girl's blond hair. He smiled, really smiled, and her heart missed a beat.

"That's wonderful, sweetheart," she said. "You did great!"

"Here, baby," Cole said, handing his daughter her bingo card. "Walk this up to the front there and show Mr. Wylie."

"Will I get a present?" she asked, her brown eyes glowing.

"If you really have a bingo." Cole turned her toward the front.

"I do," she said, taking slow, cautious steps forward as she balanced the card and the buttons covering the spaces.

The caller had stopped the game to wait for Haley.

Cole moved into Haley's vacant chair, right next to Elise. Immediately her nerve endings electrified. His shoulder brushed hers, and she practically jumped out of her skin.

"Thanks," he whispered in her ear, sending a warmth spiraling through her.

"F-for what?"

"I saw you helping her. Yet you made her feel like she'd done it all herself."

She dropped her gaze and shrugged. Cole's hand was only an inch from hers. It wouldn't take much effort for them to touch, for her to grasp his hand. Did she dare take the chance with not only his rejection but with her heart once more?

No. She'd gambled enough on love and acceptance. And she'd always lost. Having a family was enough. That's all she needed. It would give her child what she'd never had.

The clatter of a metal folding chair falling jarred them. Cole jumped out of his seat and rushed past Elise. She turned. Haley lay sprawled on the floor. Her bingo card was face down, the buttons scattered in disarray. Giant tears sprang to the little girl's eyes as she sat up.

"Da-dee!" she cried.

"Are you hurt, darlin'?" he asked, cradling her in his arms.

She shook her head and reached for the card, her shoulders shaking with sobs. "I—I w-won't win n-now."

Elise moved behind Cole and knelt beside her husband and daughter. "It's okay, Haley." She wrapped her arm around the little girl's shoulders. "They can tell by your card whether you had the spaces covered or not."

"That's right, sweetheart," Cole murmured against his daughter's hair. "Let's go show Mr. Wylie what you had. Okay?"

Snuffling against her daddy's shirt, Haley stood. Cole handed her the bingo card, and she took Elise's hand, pulling her with them.

Smiling through his half-glasses, the older man took the

card. "Let's see what we have here." He checked the card against the pieces he'd called earlier. In a moment he somberly declared into his microphone, "She's a winner, folks!"

Tears still dotting Haley's face, she beamed. "I won!"

Mr. Wylie handed her a gift-wrapped box.

Smoothing her hand over the girl's blond cap, Elise prompted her new daughter, "Say thank you."

"Thanks, Mr. Wylie." Haley hugged the box to her chest.

As Cole and Elise turned the little girl back toward their table, Mr. Wylie stopped them with, "In case any of you folks don't know, these are newlyweds. Just married a few weeks ago. Cole, why don't you introduce us to your pretty wife."

Dipping his chin in an aw-shucks manner, Cole put his hand at Elise's back, pulling her closer to him and forming a tight unit of three, with Haley standing in front of them. He cleared his throat. "This is Elise, my beautiful bride, and now Haley's mother. We feel very fortunate to have her in our family."

His words made Elise's throat tighten. How she wished that were true. But how could she ever know? How could she ever close the gap that she felt kept her and Cole apart? A gap she'd created. A gap she was scared to close for fear she'd lose everything.

After his short introduction, Cole urged them back toward their table but before they could be seated Mr. Wylie spoke again. "The congregation chipped in and bought you folks a wedding present. We've been waiting to present it to you two. Cole… Elise…y'all come on back up here."

With Haley sitting in her seat, Cole and Elise retraced their steps. Her nerves rattled together, and her knees knocked. She'd never had a present specially bought for her. Oh, she'd had Christmas presents donated to the orphanage, presents other children hadn't wanted or extra things folks had bought for a female child her age, but never a present especially picked out for her.

Mr. Wylie pulled out a decorated bag that was as big as one of Cole's fifty-pound bags of feed and handed it to Cole. "Y'all enjoy."

While holding it Cole gave a nod for her to open the package. Her heart pounding with excitement, Elise pulled out the gold-and-white tissue paper. Peering inside, she felt her breath hitch in her throat. Sudden, irrational tears seared her eyes. In only a week she'd have another birthday, but this time it wouldn't be like the lonely, quiet birthdays she'd had her whole life.

"What is it?" Cole asked, leaning close to her, his shoulder pressing against her, his hair brushing hers. His hand closed over hers and heat spread throughout her body like a wildfire. "Hey, that's great." He grinned at his daughter. "Haley, you're going to love this." He reached into the decorated bag and pulled out a wicker picnic basket. "Thanks, everybody. We'll enjoy this."

"We thought it'd make a nice family gift," Mr. Wylie concluded.

Family. The word brought tears of joy and sorrow to Elise. She'd found a family for her baby. But would she ever be a part of it? The facade they'd created seemed as fragile as spun glass.

"Now we're going to take a ten-minute refreshment break," Mr. Wylie announced, speaking into the microphone, which crackled and popped. "Y'all be sure and say howdy-do to Elise."

Chairs clattered as those around them started to move. Then a voice from the back, one that sounded suspiciously like Jack, made everyone stop with, "Kiss your bride, Cole. Before somebody else does."

Cole didn't pause. He turned toward Elise, his hand wrapping more fully around her waist, and pulled her against him, trapping her breath in her lungs. Then his mouth closed on hers, warm, determined, but with a touch of softness that turned her world upside down.

As quickly as he'd grabbed her he ended the kiss. But his hand still rested on her waist. Somehow, she drew in a thin stream of air, but her heart fluttered like a flailing bird.

Before she could break away, those around them moved forward, pumping her hand with congratulations, smiling at her, wishing her well. Names ran together. Faces became vague, unclear. Fear overwhelmed her. What if someone read through their facade? Would Cole no longer have a need for her? Would he turn her out? She felt as if she stood on quicksand. A rush of heat made her vision blur. The room tilted. By the time they were left alone, Elise's stomach rebelled.

"I'll be back." She raced to the rest room before she could embarrass herself in front of half of Desert Springs' citizens and Cole.

Amazingly, the small rest room was deserted. Drawing in gulps of much-needed air, Elise leaned over a sink and splashed water against her face. After a few moments her world settled back into place and her stomach calmed down. She dried her face with a paper towel, and then sat on a padded bench.

"You okay?" MaryAnn asked, barreling through the door.

Elise nodded. "Yes. I'm feeling better. Guess I got a little claustrophobic with everyone around us."

MaryAnn studied her a moment. "Hmm." She dampened a paper towel and blotted Elise's forehead. "They can be overwhelming. They're just so glad Cole finally found someone...decent...and nice, who'll make him happy and be a wonderful mother for Haley."

Elise gave her a doubtful look.

Clicking her tongue, MaryAnn refolded the paper towel. "His first wife was a holy terror."

"How do they know I'm not?" she asked.

"Ah, that's easy. They've seen the way you look at Cole." She pressed the cool, damp towel against Elise's forehead.

She closed her eyes, realizing MaryAnn could see the truth of how she felt about Cole. Were her emotions that easy to read? Could *he* tell?

She didn't need love. She needed a home. If love entered the picture, then everything would disintegrate and she'd be left without anything at all.

"And they can tell by the way you dote on Haley," MaryAnn continued, pushing Elise's hair away from her face. "Paula never cared about Cole, really. She always looked down at everyone here. Then when Haley was born..." She snorted with disdain. "Well, it was a downright sin the way she treated that little girl. Acted more like she was a nuisance than a precious little miracle."

"Why?" Elise asked, imagining holding her own baby in her arms in a few months. *Her* baby. Already, her heart had opened as wide as the Palo Duro Canyon with love and acceptance. She moved her hand to touch her stomach, and then stopped, not wanting to give away her secret. Not until Cole agreed it was time.

"Who knows? Frankly, I think she was just too selfish to be a mother. Did Cole tell you he had to change the baby's diapers and feed her the bottles at night?"

Elise shook her head. He had hardly spoken about his

first wife at all. It broke her heart to hear the details, to realize how Cole had suffered in silence. No wonder it had been a huge sacrifice on his part to marry again. No wonder her pregnancy had given him enormous doubts.

"Well," MaryAnn reflected, "figures Cole wouldn't say anything. Too much of a gentleman. He did pretty much everything for that sweet baby of his except give birth. And he would have done that if he could've. Paula refused to get up in the night to tend to the baby. Would've just let that newborn cry and cry. She couldn't have her beauty rest disturbed. Hell, Cole should've turned that woman over his knee and given her a good paddlin'. Still makes me so mad I could spit."

"She must have been beautiful," Elise said, "for Cole to put up with her, to have fallen in love."

MaryAnn shrugged. "I guess you could say she was beautiful. On the outside. But on the inside she was ugly as an old toad. I never did understand what Cole saw in her. But then, he's a man. And men can be lured by a sexy blonde. Lust has a way of fooling them." Then she gave a friendly wink. "Us, too, if we let it."

Elise knew a lot about lust. She'd hungered for a family. She'd desired Rusty. But she wasn't sure she knew enough about love to recognize it if it introduced itself to her. But she had an idea that if she opened her heart, Cole would fill the empty spaces inside her.

MaryAnn stood up and threw the paper towel in the trash. Reaching into her purse, she pulled out a brush and straightened Elise's hair, brushing the ends for her. "Feeling better now?"

"Yes." And no. She no longer felt ill. But she felt uncontrollable tears burning the backs of her eyes. She couldn't deny it any longer. She did care for Cole. More than she should. Because now she understood why he kept his distance.

I'm not looking for love. I simply want a wife.

The words he'd spoken the first time they met crushed her hopes. Cole would never let himself love again.

And their family would never truly be a family.

Chapter Seven

Cole inched open the door to the ladies' room. Concern dug into his nerves like barbed wire. He scanned the room until he saw Elise. She sat on a bench, leaning her head back against the wall. Her face looked pale and drawn. Her eyes remained closed. His heart hammered its way into his throat.

Searching MaryAnn's face for the answer to the question that pounded in his mind, he asked, "Is she better?"

She gave a nod and waved him inside. "She's gonna be fine."

Relief punctured holes in the hard wall of anxiety closing in on Cole. Ducking inside the rectangular room, he felt as awkward as a bridegroom on his wedding night. He knelt in front of Elise. Carefully, cautiously, he placed a hand on her knee.

Immediately her eyes opened.

"How do you feel?"

She straightened, rotating her neck from side to side. "Better."

"Was it morn—"

She touched his hand and a spark of electricity shot up his arm. Her eyes softened, glowed like moonlight. "I'm fine. Everything," she emphasized the word, "is fine."

Rubbing his palm along his jeans to erase her touch, he nodded. In a jerky movement he stood. "Good."

"You better take her on home," MaryAnn urged, interrupting the uniting moment between bride and groom. "She needs to get her rest. You take care of her, Cole. Expectant mothers are carrying precious cargo."

Cole's gaze collided with Elise's. Their secret was out. He noticed that her lip curled at the corner mischievously. He started to grin in reply but caught himself. If he confirmed MaryAnn's assumption, then the news would spread through the town grapevine like jelly.

Compressing his lips together, he glanced at MaryAnn.

She rolled her eyes and sniffed. "Claustrophobic, my foot." Then she sucked in a breath. "Oh, me and my big mouth. You've told Cole haven't you, Elise?"

She suppressed a smile. "He knows. But how did you?"

"Oh, I've owned a beauty shop long enough to have heard and seen it all. Guess y'all didn't need that honeymoon after all, eh?" MaryAnn grinned.

Not knowing what to say, how to explain, he offered his hand to Elise. "Let's go then." He put an arm around his wife's still narrow waist, relishing the feel of her against him. He'd begun to look forward to the day when her tummy would swell. "Thanks, MaryAnn, for your help."

"Anytime. Elise, take my sweater. You might need it on the way home."

"I'll bring it by your shop tomorrow," Cole said, securing the wrap over his wife's shoulders.

MaryAnn edged around them and reached for the door,

stopping before she pulled it open. "By the way," she whispered grinning, "congratulations."

Cole whisked Elise toward his truck. After he settled her in the passenger seat, he rounded up Haley. Soon they were on their way home.

Home. The word held a special new meaning for Cole now. As a boy it had been a lonely place with no brothers or sisters to play with. While married to Paula, he'd wanted to run away from the homestead that had been transformed into a cage, complete with a wife that acted like an angry tigress. After the divorce, the house had haunted him with memories. Now Elise, with her easy smile, charm and grace, had made it a retreat, a safe haven.

"Let me know if you need me to pull over," he said, glancing over at her.

The last rays of daylight slanted through the truck windows and shone on her auburn hair, glinting with fiery sparks. "I'm okay, Cole."

"Did you get sick back there?" he asked, feeling the weight of responsibility settle on his shoulders.

He hadn't felt like an expectant father in years. Suddenly the burdens, excitement and concerns of a daddy-in-waiting crashed in on him. It was probably his fault that Elise had become ill. She'd been working too hard around the ranch. From now on he'd see that she rested more. Tonight he should have made sure she ate a well-balanced dinner, not junk food. After tonight, things were going to change.

"No." she answered. "I didn't get sick. I'm fine. I just felt a little dizzy."

"Should you see a doctor?" he asked, his voice strained.

"I have been. This is normal for—" her eyes cut toward Haley "—you know."

He knew all right. Paula had said her temper tantrums were normal, too, along with the constant nausea. Would this episode of dizziness spiral Elise into a sour mood? His shoulders knotted with a new worry. Would Elise's even temper explode, targeting Haley and himself? Anxious to avoid the anguish and tyranny that reigned when his first wife became pregnant, he kept his eyes on the road and prayed.

His hands tightened on the steering wheel the rest of the way home. It was dark by the time Cole pulled into his drive. When he parked beneath the carport, he killed the engine.

"I think she's asleep," Haley whispered.

Cole glanced over his daughter's head. Elise slouched in her seat, her head tilted back, her mouth open. He smiled. "Okay, darlin'. You slide out on my side. I'll carry Elise upstairs."

Haley nodded. She took the house keys from Cole and ran ahead of him to open the door.

Wanting to tiptoe around Elise as if she were a time bomb about to go off, Cole eased his door closed and jogged around to her side of the truck. He hesitated a moment, unsure if he should touch her. He remembered all too well Paula's less-than-enthusiastic response to his touch. But, he reasoned, Elise hadn't pulled away from him earlier. In fact, she'd covered his hand with her own. His skin tightened at the memory.

Carefully, as if Elise were an egg he might crack, he eased his arm behind her back and the other under her knees. He pulled her against his chest, and she stirred.

He held his breath. Her eyelashes fluttered, her head lolled on his shoulder but she continued sleeping. Slowly he released his pent-up breath and lifted her out of the truck. Her body felt light, almost bird-like, in his arms.

The contours of her shape pressed against him, reminding him that she was all woman, with feminine curves and lines. Her softness made him hard. Her summery scent enveloped him, arousing things inside him that should not have been disturbed. When she raised her arm around his neck and snuggled against him, his heart contracted.

Only in her sleep did she need him or want him near her. As he wanted her. Maybe there was hope for their future.

By the time he'd reached their bedroom, his heart was pounding in his chest like he'd run a marathon. He nudged the door open with his elbow and turned toward Haley. "Go on and get ready for bed. I'll be there in a few minutes to tuck you in."

But first he had to tuck Elise into bed. *Oh, God.* Having to go to his daughter afterward ensured that he wouldn't linger any longer than he should at Elise's bedside. At least he hoped not.

"Is Elise gonna be okay?" Haley asked in a frightened voice, her eyes wide.

His throat cinched tight. "Sure she is. We'll take good care of her, won't we?"

Haley put his keys on the nightstand. "Should I get her some of that pink yucky medicine you make me drink when my tummy's upset?"

"No, darlin'. I think she just needs to sleep."

Standing in the pale moonlight, his daughter lifted her innocent gaze to him. "Did she eat too many hot dogs?"

He chuckled. "Maybe."

Haley nodded. "Once I ate too many corny dogs at the fair."

"That's right. As I remember you ate a cupcake, a candied apple and a bag of cotton candy just before you rode on the merry-go-round a few times. But it didn't take too long for you to get better.''

She gave him a toothy grin and started to leave the room. At the door she stopped and turned back. ''Does Elise like living here with us, Daddy?''

The raw pain in his child's face nearly brought him to his knees. Haley knew her mother had hated living with them. Paula had made it all too clear. He prayed silently that Elise would find what she was looking for here on the ranch with them, and that nothing would take her away.

He vowed then that he'd make sure Elise was happy here. No matter what. For his daughter's sake.

But he knew it was for his own sake, as well.

''Yes, baby, I think she's happy living with us. Now go on to your room.'' God, he hoped so. He couldn't bear it if she left. And he knew his daughter would be crushed as well.

''G'night, Elise,'' she whispered, touching her new momma's limp leg. Then she turned and went down the hall to her room.

When he heard the doorknob click closed, he drew in a deep, steadying breath. Moonlight cast shadows and pearly light about the room. He moved toward the bed. Suddenly his hands felt sweaty, his knees weak. *This is ridiculous! Get a grip, Dalton.*

Feeling the muscles in his back strain, he bent and gently laid Elise along the mattress. The pillow cushioned her head. His face remained inches from hers, his mouth so close he could have kissed her. If he'd wanted to.

But he shouldn't. Not now. Not like this.

When he kissed Elise again, really kissed her, he wanted it to be special. He wanted her to remember. The way he remembered their wedding kiss. Dammit, he wanted it to drive her wild, for her to want him as badly as he wanted her. But he wouldn't beg. He wouldn't ask for something she wasn't willing to give.

He hesitated a moment too long. Before he pulled back, Elise opened her eyes. The hazel orbs looked foggy and confused as she stared at him. She blinked twice, and then recognition dawned. A gleam made her eyes sparkle and crinkle at the corners.

"Cole," she whispered, her breath grazing his lips.

His gut clenched. "I'm here," he reassured her, sounding hoarse, "if you need me."

Leave, Dalton. Now. Before it's too late. Slowly, he closed his fingers around her arms and started to pull away from her. She tightened her hold on him and sifted her fingers through the hair at the back of his neck. A flame burned in his belly.

"Wait," she said. "Please."

"Elise…"

She lifted her mouth to his, closed that intimate space, shut off his sanity. He tasted her sweet breath first, sucked in air like a drowning man and willingly gave up the fight.

Her lips were pliable and melded with his. She opened to him, pulled him inside her, demanded and took as much as he'd taken from her on their wedding day. She arched her back and her breasts pressed into his chest. The firm mounds erased the last bit of logic in his brain.

The kiss turned eager, greedy. He gathered her into his arms again. His one last conscious thought, before he died and went to heaven, was that he should stop this insanity. Elise didn't know what she was doing. She was ill and therefore vulnerable.

Damn. That one thought doused his desire. With one last grab for resistance he pushed away and cursed himself for being a fool.

"G'night, Elise," he said in a strangled voice. "Sweet dreams."

He'd have steamy ones. If he managed to fall asleep...after another cold shower.

That was some invitation, Elise! Have you lost your mind?

Possibly. She blinked against the blackness that surrounded her. Cole had roused her from a warm, safe dream. At first she thought she'd been imagining the warmth of his embrace, the security of his arms. But his heat had penetrated her sleep, stirred needs and desires that were too real for a dream.

She hadn't wanted it to end. This time, he hadn't kissed her. He hadn't made the first move. She had. She'd kissed him, fully, completely, without any reservations. What had she done? *Oh, Lord!*

She flung her feet over the side of the bed and stood. Her knees felt rubbery, her head woozy. Was it the baby making her feel as if her stomach had been turned inside out? Or was it Cole's kiss? She preferred to think it was her pregnancy.

Unable to escape the truth pounding in her breast, she moved to the window and stared out at the starlit sky. So many times as a child she'd wished upon a star, hoping and praying that her wishes would come true—that she'd be given a family of her own.

Now she had one.

And it wasn't enough.

She turned her back on the stars and her misconstrued, childhood fantasies. A chill swept through her body. Cole had rejected her kiss. He'd rejected *her*.

Her gaze shifted to the wide, empty bed. A tremor ripped through her body, and she shivered. Her heart began to shrivel. Now she'd have no one to keep her warm, to keep her safe, to care about her and love her. She'd be alone again.

"I'm going to the barbershop," Cole stated, as he rinsed his breakfast dishes in the sink.

Earlier than usual, he'd taken Haley to start her last week of school. His baby was growing up so fast. When he'd returned, Elise had greeted him with a breakfast hardy enough for the entire Dallas Cowboy offensive line.

"Since you're going to town, would you mind taking MaryAnn's sweater back?" Elise asked, pushing back from the table.

"Sure." He opened the dishwasher.

"Don't worry about the dishes. I'll take care of them."

"I don't mind." He wanted her to get plenty of rest.

"But it's my job," she protested, carrying her plate to the counter.

He noticed the dark circles under her eyes. "Your job is to rest and take care of yourself. I don't want what happened Saturday night to happen again."

The corners of her mouth turned downward. "Is that why you took Haley to school this morning?"

He nodded. "You don't have to be her chauffeur. Or our personal chef and housekeeper." He grasped her shoulders, felt her fragile bones beneath his palms. "We're a family. Not a business. Take care of yourself."

Her eyes immediately filled with tears and his heart crumbled. What had he said? What did he do? Had he somehow insulted her? He knew she wanted to feel needed. She'd cried after her meat loaf disaster—afraid she wouldn't make a good wife and mother. Seeing tears well in her eyes and her proud chin quiver, he had an urge to pull her against his chest and comfort her. But did he dare?

What else could he do? Cursing himself for hurting her, he wrapped his arms around her and breathed in her sleepy scent that did more to arouse him than a bucket of cold water dumped on his head could diminish. "What's wrong? What did I say?"

She shook her head. "Nothing." Snuffling against his shoulder, she said, "Nobody's ever cared enough to look out for me...to worry about me...or my baby."

That's all it was, Elise told herself. Cole didn't love her. He was simply concerned for the baby. But that was enough to bring tears and to rip open her heart.

Awkwardly, Cole patted her shoulders and then slowly eased away from her with a tender kiss placed carefully on her forehead. "Why don't you go get some rest? You look tired."

She was. She hadn't slept well in weeks, realizing now that it wasn't because Cole slept in the same room, but because he slept so far away from her. She wanted to snuggle against him, to feel his strong arms around her. But she didn't dare ask. She couldn't stand being rejected by him...again.

"I'll be watching to see if it takes nine full months." Annelle Wittlefield spoke loudly over the whir of the hair dryer.

Cole came to a halt in the doorway of MaryAnn's Cut and Curl. The tips of his ears burned. What the hell? Did everyone in town already know?

The door swung shut behind him and popped him on the backside. Above his head, bells jangled. Then an unnatural quiet descended on the gossips gathered. No one snipped, brushed or uttered a word. Cole cursed beneath his breath and set his mouth in a grim, determined line. Better he face the condemnation than Elise.

Darla Brown, her hair sprouting through a plastic cap like she was a retro punk rocker, coughed, trying to signal Annelle. Beth Thompson, a clerk at the Piggly Wiggly, looked like her eyes had swallowed her face. LouEllen Masters, the owner of the only dry cleaners within a thirty-mile radius, covered her mouth with her hand.

Only the whir of the dryer covering her gray hair like a beehive prevented the busiest busybody in Desert Springs from noticing his sudden appearance. "I'll bet you a dollar for donuts," Annelle continued, "that she delivers early. Just how early," she said shifting her wide frame in the blue, plastic-covered chair, "we'll have to wait and see."

Cole's hand crushed MaryAnn's pink sweater. He let the door bang shut and stalked through the row of barber chairs, ignoring the preacher's wife's last comment.

Mrs. Wittlefield's mouth opened, but she recovered quickly. "Well, howdy-do, Cole."

He stopped at Sally Macon's station, and the women started to circle him like buzzards, ready to pick him to pieces.

"Elise sure is a pretty li'l thing."

"Congratulations, Cole."

"Y'all sure were in a hurry to get married."

"Didn't you want a church wedding?"

He ignored the questions and comments fired at him and spoke directly to the hairstylist. "Where's MaryAnn?"

Sally tilted her head toward the sinks lining the far wall. "In back."

He gave a curt nod and stalked away.

"Now don't go blaming MaryAnn," Sally called after him. "She didn't say nothin'. You know she can keep a secret better than a skeleton."

He entered the back area where MaryAnn was pushing towels into an industrial-sized washer. "You'd have thought we bought a home pregnancy test at the Piggly Wiggly.''

MaryAnn turned. Her brow crinkled then she smiled. "I knew it wouldn't take the ladies long to figure out what was wrong with Elise last night." She poured a generous helping of detergent into the washer. "How is she today?"

"Better."

"Well, don't worry. The ladies gotta have something to talk about. What else is there to do here besides watch soaps and play bridge? You and Elise happen to be the latest, most interesting morsel of gossip. Probably a lot more titillating for them than the latest Bo and Hope drama on *One Life to Live*. Next week, something else will catch their attention."

He scuffed his boot in frustration. "Not unless the preacher's caught having an affair, or a tornado blows away half the town."

MaryAnn brushed back a lock of bleached blond hair. "Well, neither is likely. So get used to being the local star for the moment."

"You mean star, or villain?" he asked, tension pressuring the nerves along his shoulder blades.

"You could never be seen as a bad guy in this town, Cole. You're too well-respected and loved." She pushed a hand towel into the batch. "Just remember, by the time Elise has your baby, they won't be counting dates anymore."

He scowled. *Your baby.*

It wasn't *his.* That fact gnawed at him. For some odd reason he wished it were. Not because he didn't want to help raise a kid that wasn't a blood relation. He simply wished he and Elise shared that intimate bond. Hell, he wished he'd had the chance of getting her pregnant. He hated the reminder that someone else—some cowboy named Rusty—had been with Elise. That it was *his* baby she was carrying. Damn. He shouldn't care. But he did.

"You know the women in this town better than that," he said, trying not to reveal his turbulent emotions. "They might forget for a while. But the moment the baby arrives they'll start counting backwards."

MaryAnn started the washer and a whoosh of water swirled onto the load of towels. "What do you care? I mean, what if she did get pregnant *before* you got married? That's not exactly headline news. Even round these parts."

Which was worse, he wondered, Haley learning her parents *had* to get married or being told their marriage was a facade? Time to change the subject. Trying to guard his daughter made his head pound. Imagining his daughter's reaction made his heart ache.

It wouldn't be easy on him or Elise, either. But he wasn't worried about himself. He realized then that he cared a whole lot more for Elise than he'd anticipated. Somehow, she made him want to protect her, whether it was her reputation or her life.

"Here's your sweater," he said, feeling uncomfortable, as if his own clothes didn't fit right anymore. "Thanks again for your help the other night."

"My pleasure. I like Elise." She patted his arm and offered him an encouraging smile. "She's a wonderful catch. For you and for Haley."

"I think so." At least for his daughter's benefit she'd be a good mother. But with him—hell, she'd managed to tie him into a tangle of knots. "I better be getting back."

She nodded. "Tell Elise hello and to keep crackers or some hard candy on hand for when she starts feeling queasy again."

"That helps?" he asked, not wanting to see her sick anymore.

"That's what they say." Giving him a warm hug, she added, "Congrats, Papa Bear. Jack and I are so happy for you. For all of you."

Cole gave a nod, his throat tight. They'd stood by him through so much over the past few years.

"We'll see you Friday night." She gave a slight wave.

He lifted one eyebrow in question.

"You're bringing Haley by about seven," she answered his silent question.

"I am? We are? Does Elise know about this?"

"Not yet." She lifted her chin defiantly. "And don't you argue with me."

A cold knot formed in his stomach. "About what?"

She grinned mischievously. "Haley's gonna spend the night with Jack and me."

"What's the occasion?"

"Your one month anniversary. And Saturday is Elise's birthday."

"It is? She told you that?"

"No. I saw it on your marriage certificate. Didn't you know?

"No."

"Men." She turned him around and gave him a shove toward the front of the shop and the gossip sharks. "Now go buy her a nice present and get ready to take your bride out for a nice dinner. I want you two to enjoy the evening...and night alone."

Chapter Eight

The cat was out of the bag. Now, Cole had to tell his daughter before the rumors reached her friends at school. He held Elise's hand tightly, presenting a united front, and entered Haley's bedroom. At least Elise wanted to help him. Her presence at his side gave him some much-needed reassurance. His nerves crackled, ready to snap. His heart stretched in different directions. He'd married Elise to give his daughter a mother. Now he had to turn his daughter's world upside down again by telling her news that most children dreaded hearing.

"Uh-oh," Haley said, looking up from her doll collection. "I didn't mean to do it. It was an accident."

Cole raised an eyebrow. "What are you talking about?"

Haley's eyes widened. "Nothing." She pursed her lips and turned away, pretending to rock her doll to sleep.

Suspicious, Cole wondered what he should say now—if he should pursue it. Should he force his daughter to confess? But to what? This parenting job had more questions than answers.

"You mean the cookie-jar lid?" Elise asked.

His daughter nodded slowly, and then she whirled round. "It slipped outa my hand—"

"I fixed it," Elise interrupted.

"You did?" Haley's frozen features melted into a smile.

"It's good as new." Elise put her arm around Haley's ttle shoulders. "Don't be afraid to tell me things like that. verybody has accidents. Most can be fixed with the right ind of glue. Okay?"

"Okay!" Haley grinned, and put her doll into the pink assinet.

Elise tapped Haley on top of the head. "But about those issing cookies..." She smiled down at Cole's daughter ffectionately. "Did you brush your teeth after your nack?"

Haley slanted her gaze toward Elise. "Yeah."

"Yes, ma'am," Cole corrected.

"To hide the evidence, huh?" Elise chuckled.

"Are you about ready for bed, darlin'?"

Haley bounded onto her four-poster bed, making the prings creak. "Can't I stay up a little longer?"

"Nope. Cookie monsters have to get their rest." And e couldn't put this off any longer.

"Can you and Elise read me a really long story, then?" ler eyes brightened.

"Not tonight, honey," Elise said, sitting on the edge of e comforter. She'd insisted they tell Haley the news, now at it was all over town. She pulled the covers over Ha-y's legs. "We wanted to talk to you about something."

His daughter tilted her head to the side, and her gaze ettled on Cole. A cold lump of dread formed in his stom-ch.

"About the baby?" she asked.

Elise glanced at him. Surprise and confusion furrow
her brow.

"You know?" he asked, sitting beside Elise, one ha
on her shoulder. The other one reached for Haley, wanti
to help her through this moment, to understand that l
love for her would never waver.

"Sure." She shrugged. "Everybody was talkin' abo
it the night Elise got sick."

Elise rolled her eyes heavenward, and Cole swallow
a groan. Now his daughter would probably resent them
not telling her first.

"How do you feel about it, sweetheart?" Elise ask
probing gently.

Haley shrugged. "Is it a girl or a boy?"

"We don't know yet," Cole answered. He shifted l
gaze toward Elise. "Do we?"

She gave him a secretive smile that made his nerve e
ings tingle. "No, we don't know." Elise focused on Hal
"Does it matter to you if it's a boy or a girl?"

"Well," Haley drawled, "boys are kinda yucky."

"What about Tommy Davidson?" Elise asked.

Haley giggled. "He's sorta cute, I guess."

"Does that mean you like him?" Elise grinned.

"No way! He's not my boyfriend or nothin'."

"Boyfriend!" Cole felt as if he'd blinked and miss
half his daughter's life. "You are way too young—"

"Daddy!" Haley protested.

"Cole, it's all right." Elise put her hand on his thigl
His skin electrified and his nerve endings jumped li
they were live wires. Everything was *not* all right. Not
his daughter was old enough to notice boys. And not if
couldn't get his concentration off Elise.

"What about a little sister?" Elise changed the subj
back to the important topic.

"Like in Cinderella?" Haley asked, her voice suddenly trembling. She wadded a fistful of blanket in her hands.

Confused, Cole shook his head, deferring to Elise.

"You mean like those mean old stepsisters?" she asked. Elise apparently understood his daughter better than he did. A spark of jealousy ignited inside Cole, but he snuffed it out quickly. That was the reason he'd wanted a wife—someone to share the burden of parenting with, someone who could understand his little girl.

Pouting, Haley nodded.

Elise wrapped her arms around his daughter and pulled her close. "Oh, sweetheart. Why would you think that?"

"Tamara Watson said—"

"It doesn't matter what she said," Cole interjected, disliking the comparison with the fairy tale. He never had liked that nosy kid Tamara. "She doesn't know Elise, does she?"

Haley shook her head back and forth.

Elise cupped the little girl's face with the palm of her hand. "You don't think I'm like that stepmother in Cinderella who made her do all those chores, do you?"

"No way!" Haley's sudden defense reminded him of his own protectiveness toward Elise.

He choked on a ball of emotion. He'd wanted this for so long. It hadn't worked with Paula. He hadn't been enough as a single parent. But now, with Elise, they were forming a family.

"Then," Elise said, lifting Haley's face and gently smoothing back her hair, "your baby sister—"

"Or brother," Cole added with a smile. His heart warmed to the idea that maybe he'd be granted his wish—maybe someday they'd have a house full of children.

Elise smiled. "—won't be anything like those silly fairy tales."

"Really?" She looked up at Elise, her eyes widening with hope.

"Really." Elise gave her a kiss on the cheek and helped Haley settle back into her bed. "Now, you get some sleep. We can talk about this tomorrow. Maybe you can help us come up with some names for the baby. Okay?"

"Okay." Haley kissed them both good-night and then scrunched down into her covers and closed her eyes.

After they turned out the lights, Haley said, "Next time y'all do something like this, you can tell me. You don' have to hide it. All right?"

"It's a deal," Elise said. Smiling, she took Cole's hand and pulled him from the room.

Cole wondered what he'd done to be so lucky to have such a wonderful daughter and a beautiful, caring wife. She made talking to Haley so easy, so natural. How did she always know the right thing to say?

"You're amazing, you know that?" he said as they walked down the hall toward their room.

"How's that?" The look she gave him was full of hope, full of—something he couldn't identify.

He lifted his shoulders awkwardly. "You always know what to say to her."

"No, I don't. I just listen to what she's saying and respond. So do you."

Did he? He always felt like he was about to topple of a jagged cliff. He had the same feeling now, as he stared into Elise's sultry hazel eyes.

What was happening to him? Was he starting to love his wife? In a way he liked the idea, just like his great-great-grandfather had come to love his mail-order bride. After all, he wanted the marriage to last. But, at the same time, it scared the hell out of him.

It was one thing to care for Elise. It was a whole othe

thing to fall in love with her. He let go of her hand. "We need to talk."

"About what?" Elise asked, her smile fading as she mirrored his serious tone. They stood in the middle of the hall, a few scant feet from their bedroom.

"MaryAnn offered to watch Haley this Friday night so we could celebrate our one-month anniversary."

"Oh," Elise said cautiously, carefully hiding her reaction.

He wondered if it unsettled her as much as it did him. He wondered if she felt the same magnetic pull, the same paralyzing fear. "Well, I couldn't say no." He stared down at the rounded toe of his boot. He couldn't say the words clogging his throat. He *wanted* to be alone with her. Plain and simple. But it wasn't simple—it was complicated as hell. "I mean, that would have caused questions. So I agreed."

When he glanced back at her, a range of varying emotions crossed her face, and he couldn't decipher them fast enough to gauge her reaction. He braced himself for a version of one of Paula's temper tantrums.

"In other words, in a roundabout way, you're asking me out on a date."

Confused by the way she'd twisted his words, he said, "I guess we do have to go out. Unless you don't want to...or don't feel up to it." He shoved his hands into his jeans pockets. "You didn't have any other plans, did you?"

"No." Her lips pressed tight. She turned on her heel and walked into the bedroom, her back stiff.

More confused now than he was after experiencing one of her kisses, he called after her, "Was that 'no' you didn't have plans, or 'no' you don't want to go?"

With a sigh, she turned to face him. He expected anger

but instead read hurt in her eyes. His stomach wa
clenched as tightly as she grip on the doorknob. "I gues:
I have plans now."

"What did I say?"

"Nothing," she answered, and shut the door. The knob
clicked softly, but to his ears it sounded like a bolt slam
ming. What had he done now?

In two steps he reached the door and jerked it open
Elise stood by the dresser, her hand pressed to her heart
"What was that supposed to mean?" he asked. "What wa
I supposed to say? How are we supposed to have a rela
tionship if you won't discuss anything with me?"

"A relationship!" She gave a harsh laugh. "You hav
a better relationship with that horse of yours. You neve
ask me anything. You tell. You order. You say we're goin;
to town to play bingo. Now, we have to go out Friday
night to celebrate. Well, whoopee! What a celebration."

He felt the sting of her words like a slap across his face

She drew in a shaky breath. "I'm sorry, Cole.
shouldn't have said that."

He sank onto the edge of the bed. "I'm glad you did
You're right. I didn't handle this well. Hell, I haven't han
dled our marriage well." He plowed his fingers throug!
his hair. His stomach contracted with a sudden case o
nerves. "Look, Elise, I really would like to spend mor
time with you...with my wife. Alone. Would you like t
go out Friday night and celebrate our anniversary?"

"Yes," she smiled shyly, "I'd like that."

"You look like Cinderella!" Haley exclaimed a fev
days later.

"At least you didn't say the mean old stepmother,'
Elise said, feeling heat rise along her neck and burn he
cheeks. What was she doing?

Her stomach lurched. This time she knew it didn't have anything to do with the baby. It only had to do with Cole.

Oh, Elise, you've done it now. You have really bungled this whole thing! Not only did she want to go out with Cole tonight, but she wanted it to be a date. A *real* date. With compliments and stolen kisses. That might lead to something else at the end of the evening, something rare and intimate. But Cole obviously didn't want any of the things she wanted. Hadn't she offered herself to him the other night? He'd kissed her and walked out the door.

Oh, Lord! She was living in a fairy tale if she thought her dream could come true. More than likely she was heading up the road to "Heartbreak Hotel."

"You're radiant," MaryAnn added with a pleased smile. She held a can of hair spray in one hand and a brush in the other. "Cole will be the envy of every man in Amarillo. I won't be surprised if he has to punch out a few cowpokes to keep them away from you."

"I doubt that," Elise said with a wary eye on the oval mirror in the corner of her bedroom. Tonight she wanted to look sexy, not like an expectant mommy. She tried to suck in her tummy but still she looked bloated.

MaryAnn had tried her best. She'd swept her hair up on top of her head for a glamorous do. Curly tendrils grazed Elise's nape. Not only had her new friend styled her hair and let her borrow a white dress accented with silver studs and fringe, but MaryAnn had also given her a pair of sterling earrings that dangled and bobbed, caught the light and sparkled like fairy dust. She twirled in front of the mirror and watched as the handkerchief skirt flared at the bottom, showing off her new white leather boots.

"I wanna be just like you when I grow up." Haley stared up at her, adoration shining in her eyes.

An overpowering emotion, a joy she'd never known,

never dreamed existed, tightened around her heart. As a little girl she'd wondered what love felt like. Now she knew. A warm, comforting sensation flooded her heart.

At the same time, responsibility clamped like a vise on her shoulders. She had much to live up to, even more to pay back for this incredible gift. She wanted to be the best mother she could be for Haley's sake. But there was so much she didn't know, so much that could go wrong.

Her hand touched her abdomen. Soon she'd have her very own child. She'd thought at one time that it would be her only family. Now she knew the family she'd longed for would include Haley, too. Never had she felt so blessed, so indebted to someone. For Haley had been the first to love her. And Cole had made it all possible. Tears burned her eyes, and she blinked until they evaporated. If only Cole could love her. If only he wanted to love her as much as she wanted to love him.

"Thanks, MaryAnn," she said, her voice hoarse with emotion. This wonderful woman had accepted her into the community, rejoiced that she'd married Cole and believed that she'd make a good mother to a hurting little girl. "I appreciate the help. I certainly need it lately. You should have done my hair for the wedding, too."

"Ah, you didn't need my help, sugar. You had the twinkle of love in your eye."

More like the glimmer of panic, Elise thought.

"And now you have that special glow."

MaryAnn zipped a pouch stuffed full of hair accessories, combs and brushes. "Expectant mommies need special treatment." She smoothed a hand over Haley's head. "And you have a wonderful new mommy, don't you sweetie?"

"Uh-huh," Haley replied, grinning. "Did you know she made my favorite this week?"

"Chocolate chip cookies?" MaryAnn asked, lifting her brows in mock surprise. "And you didn't save me any?"

Haley giggled. "They all went to school."

"Almost all." Elise tickled Haley until she squealed. Wild, unfamiliar emotions flooded her heart. She wished she'd had a mother to share memories. But now she had a daughter, and her life felt more complete than ever before. "Except for the ones I'd hidden in the cookie jar that mysteriously disappeared. Next time we'll have to make a special batch just for MaryAnn, won't we, Haley?"

"Tomorrow?" Haley asked, exuberant.

Elise's throat tightened. Making cookies with her new daughter would be the best birthday present she'd ever received. Even if no one knew it was her special day, even if no one cared. It would be one of the happiest birthdays of her life, just spending it with this precious little girl.

"Come on, sweetie," MaryAnn announced, grabbing the little girl's hand. "We need to be going. We'll make cookies at my house tonight. Your momma has a date."

"Mommies and daddies don't date," Haley declared with a frown.

"Sure they do." MaryAnn smiled at Elise. "Y'all have fun. And don't worry about rushing over in the morning to pick Haley up. We'll be fine. Y'all sleep in late. Enjoy yourselves." She gave her a broad wink.

Elise's stomach flip-flopped. A date. With Cole. The idea twisted her nerves into knots. What would they talk about? What would they do?

Women. Who could figure them out?

Cole certainly couldn't. He paced the entryway waiting for Elise to finish getting ready for their "date." He couldn't think of their evening as a date, even though he thought of Elise as a woman he wanted to date.

Haley had left with MaryAnn over thirty minutes earlier. What was keeping Elise? They were going to be late for their dinner reservations. He'd thought of making it a birthday celebration, since MaryAnn had told him about Elise's birthday, but had decided Haley would want to be included, too. Tonight they'd focus on each other, on their marriage, and try to form a bridge that would lead them into a brighter future.

Turning himself toward the stairs he took them two at a time. His pace didn't slow until he reached his closed bedroom door. He hesitated, and then decided to knock. "Elise?"

Through the wood he heard the rustling of clothes, the shuffling of shoes. There was a long pause before she said, "Come in."

When he entered the room, Elise had her back to him. She wore a loose top and black leggings that followed the contours of her legs. She reached into the laundry basket and folded one of his T-shirts.

He rephrased the we're-going-to-be-late exclamation that had been swirling around his head. "Um, can I help you do this later? We need to be going."

"I've changed my mind." Her voice sounded muffled and strained.

That stopped him midstride. Then he saw the dress MaryAnn had brought discarded on the chair in the corner, covered in a plastic bag. "About tonight? Why?"

She didn't look up from her task. "It's not necessary as long as everyone *thinks* we're going out. We don't really have to."

"I didn't think about it that way." Or maybe he hadn't *wanted* to contemplate that angle. Fact was, he *wanted* to go out with Elise. He wanted an excuse to spend time with her, to hear her laughter, to watch the corners of her eyes crinkle when she smiled. He wasn't sure he wanted to admit the disappointment pinching him at the moment.

Confused, he asked, "Are you sick?"

"No."

"You feel okay, then?"

"I'm fine."

He sat on the edge of the bed, unsure what to do or say now. "I thought I apologized for..."

She shook her head. "It's not that. It's just...well, I backed you into a corner. I realize now that you didn't really want to go out. You were forced. I did the same thing that I accused you of doing."

As she started to turn away, he touched her arm. She looked at him then, and he saw the shine on her nose and her red-rimmed eyes.

Had she been crying? What an insensitive clod he'd turned out to be. "Are you okay?"

"I told you," she said, pulling away, "I'm fine." Her voice sounded controlled, but he noticed her hands trembling.

"Don't shut me out. Not again. Talk to me, Elise. I can't read your mind."

She drew in a shuddering breath, and he thought she was going to bawl. But she didn't. She squared her shoulders instead and looked him right in the eye. "It's not your fault. You didn't do anything wrong."

"Then what?" When she didn't speak, he added, "Can't we be friends?"

"Friends?" She jerked away from him. "Half the time you act like you don't want to be around me. How can we be friends?"

He felt like he'd been sucker-punched. The air went out of his lungs with a whoosh. "Don't want you?" He started to laugh but stopped himself. The absurdity of the situation amazed him. Then anger flared like a gasoline-soaked match. "Are you crazy? You're the one who said we couldn't...couldn't..." His gaze shifted toward the bed. "You know."

"You made it clear the other night you didn't want to go out with me." Her voice cracked but anger burned in the depths of her hazel eyes. "You were only doing it because others expected it. It's obvious you don't want me."

"Want you? Hell, I want you so badly it hurts."

His voice resounded in the confines of the room. Then silence throbbed between them. Her breath came hard and fast in sync with the driving beat of his heart. He realized then he'd jumped off the cliff. There was no going back.

"You're all I can think about. All I dream about, Elise."

She shook her head, her eyes wide with disbelief. "You want me?"

He pulled her closer, wedging her body against his. "Hell, yes."

"Me?" Denial rang in her voice. She blinked back a rush of tears.

"No one else but you." She stared at him, amazement opening her heart to possibilities.

"You really don't know do you? You can't see how desirable you are?"

"I guess I never felt...good enough."

"Well, you are. Good enough to eat." He dipped his head, tasted a salty tear and whispered against her ear, "I can still taste you, feel you. I've never felt this way about anyone. I've never wanted anyone so much. I've—"

Without another thought, she put a hand on his chest stopping him from finishing his next sentence. Then she kissed him, kissed him with a devouring, consuming desire that matched his own. With one hand behind his head and one clutching the front of his shirt, she melded her body with his and held him. He realized at that moment she'd already imprisoned his heart.

He tasted her mouth, sampled what could be between them if only she would let it happen. He sensed she wanted more, more than he could offer—his heart.

The idea of loving her scared the hell out of him. His first instinct was to panic. But if he did, he knew he would hurt her again. And possibly lose her.

Slowly, tenderly, he cupped her jaw and ended the kiss, nibbling at the corners of her mouth. One last taste, that's all he wanted. But he knew it would never be enough. "You look beautiful tonight."

She tried to look away, but he held her face in his hands. He willed his eyes to speak what he couldn't say with words. Could she see inside his soul? Into his heart? Could she see what he wanted to promise but didn't dare?

"Now, let me take you to dinner. Before…before I do something to jeopardize the agreement we made."

"Forget the agreement!" Elise wanted to scream. But she couldn't. Her heart lodged in her throat as Cole's words swirled in her head. *I want you so badly it hurts.*

Giddy as a schoolgirl, she felt as if she'd just plucked the petals off a daisy and ended with "He loves me!" She'd even changed back into MaryAnn's dress.

But reality fizzled the joy in her soul. Cole didn't love her. He only wanted her in his bed, as Rusty had. After her ex-boyfriend had enjoyed what he'd wanted, he'd tossed her aside. All too well, she knew the painful difference between love and lust. She wouldn't jeopardize their marriage or her heart.

Sobered by her own sore memories, she stiffly walked

down the stairs. She paused on the last step, her gaze landing on Cole and the picnic basket. "Aren't we going out?"

He gave a shy grin. "I started to think about those reservations in Amarillo. And the fact that I really didn't want to share you with a roomful of strangers. I thought maybe we should stay home. Spend some time alone. Without any interruptions."

She gripped the banister. "What?"

He moved toward her, settling his hands on her waist and sending shivers of pure pleasure along her heated skin. Even though she was standing on a step above him, he still towered over her. Instead of staring at his wide expanse of shoulders, she tilted her head back to look into his eyes. Was that longing she saw? Desire? Or was there more?

God, how she wanted to believe there was more than lust.

"B-but I thought this was all for show...to celebrate our anniversary," she stammered, her nerves jumbled by his touch, by his suggestion.

He shook his head. "Let's celebrate. But here. Alone. In private."

"But, Cole—"

"I'm not asking for anything else, Elise. I just simply want to be alone with you, my wife. I don't want you to think I'm pretending because of others. When I hold your hand, when I slip my arm around your waist and kiss your neck, it's not a show. It's just you and me. That's all. I don't want to be around anyone else. I don't want any distractions. I just want you."

His words overwhelmed her, touched a place in her heart that had been aching for a long while. Before she could rethink their "date" and question the wisdom of it,

Cole stepped away, held out his hand for her and walked her to the door.

They stepped out on the porch together, and the warm summery breeze drifted over her. In the time she'd gotten dressed again, he'd strung white Christmas lights around the posts and placed a thick blanket on the planks. He set the picnic basket in the middle and helped her to sit down.

"I didn't have much time to prepare anything." Concern lined his forehead. "So I hope you like chicken salad and cantaloupe."

"Perfect," she said, knowing it would be her favorite meal for years to come. Because Cole had made it for her. Just for her.

The twinkling Christmas lights cast a romantic glow over their makeshift table. Was he trying to seduce her? Or was he simply being sweet and attentive? Her distrust of men warred with her need to believe in Cole. She tried not to notice the sharp angles of his tanned face, the warm glow of interest in his gaze, the gentle curve of his mouth that could be both hard and soft, demanding and delicious.

"How about some bottled water?" he asked, pausing between bites. "Chilled to perfection. It's a lovely vintage of spring water."

She smiled then, feeling her heart lighten. "Sounds wonderful."

As he poured the water into wine glasses, he slid a glance toward her. "Are you sure this is all right? Or did you want to go to a fancy restaurant?" He paused and handed her the glass. "We can still make our reservations, if that's what you want."

She nodded. "This is perfect. A dream come true."

"Are you too warm out here? I could turn the fan on."

"I'm fine." His concern touched her.

"I've heard you say that before. But you weren't, then."

Maybe he was paying closer attention than she'd thought, more so than anyone had ever bothered. A trace of a smile touched her lips. She longed to be known, inside and out, intimately by one person—by Cole. Would he ever care enough to search out her secrets?

Blood tumbled through her veins like white rapids rushing over rocks. But in a surprisingly cool tone, she asked the question burning inside her, "What exactly do you want out of our marriage, Cole?"

He sipped his water and swallowed, thoughtfully. As he handed her a paper plate and crackers, he answered, "I thought I made that clear from the beginning."

A sharp pain stabbed her heart. "So, you just want sex. Is that it?"

How had she done it again? She'd fallen for a cowboy just like Rusty who only wanted a good time and no real intimacy.

"I wouldn't say that." He placed several sliced wedges of cheese on her plate followed by a mound of chicken salad. "But I don't deny it, either." The twinkling lights glimmered in the depths of his eyes. "I think at one time that's all I wanted out of a relationship...out of our marriage. But not anymore. I like the fact that we can share in the responsibility of parenting, that we can discuss Haley, and someday the baby, together." He sighed wearily as if he'd carried a heavy load. "I want companionship. That's what was missing in my first marriage."

"You and..." She hesitated trying to remember his first wife's name.

"Paula," he supplied.

She nodded. "Paula. She...you...y'all—"

"You could say we didn't get along." His mouth tightened into a straight line. "But then Paula didn't get along ith many people. She hated it here. Hated the ranch. ated being pregnant. I think she even came to hate me.''

"Why?"

He shrugged. "She didn't like the isolation, the loneli- ess of the ranch. She thought the folks in Desert Springs ere hillbillies. She saw them as caricatures, not people. he didn't want to get pregnant. It was an accident.'' His oice dropped to a hoarse whisper. "She wanted to… rminate…'' His jaw hardened. "She didn't want to have y baby.''

A jolt of outrage struck Elise. She saw anger simmering elow Cole's barely controlled features. She felt his pain nd horror in her own soul. "How did you change her ind?"

He rubbed his jaw. "I promised her we'd move."

"Move? Away from your home? Where?"

"Anywhere she wanted. I was desperate. I promised her d sell the ranch.''

That would have been a slow suicide for Cole because e loved his ranch, his heritage.

He took a bite of chicken salad and when he swallowed, e said, "By the time Haley was old enough for us to onsider moving, Paula had decided to move…to move on ithout us. She wanted her freedom more than she wanted ur family.''

The pain in his voice touched her, moved her in ways e'd never imagined. He'd been rejected, too. He knew e deep agony, anger and self-loathing. She felt a sudden inship with Cole on a deeper level than parenting.

It brought her to a brink of desperation, where she had ask the inevitable. She had to know how he felt about aula because it would tell her so much. If he could ever ove beyond that relationship to love someone else. "Did ou love her?''

He took his time answering, and Elise's heart pound
out every second he delayed.

"At one time. It was foolish really. We were young. V
met while I was showing horses in Dallas. She though
cattle ranch sounded romantic. Hell, I don't think I v
thinking at all. We should have taken the time to get
know each other better. But we didn't. We jumped i
marriage. And then we regretted it. By the time she I
us, I don't think I'd loved her for a long time. But I v
committed to the relationship. She wasn't though." I
shoved his fingers through his hair, making tufts stand
end. "She wasn't easy to love. She didn't make it easy

Elise knew she'd never been easy to love, either. Tha
what the nuns had said in the orphanage. Parents looki
to adopt a child had made it crystal clear that she was
lovable. And now Cole…

"Is that what you're looking for?" Cole asked, leani
forward, reaching for her hand. "Love?"

Her throat clamped shut and her heart crumpled into ti
pieces. She pulled away from him and averted her ga
How could she voice her deepest desire, her aching nee
With false bravado, she answered, "How can I miss wl
I've never had?"

Liar! Of course she wanted love. She'd dreamed of
while watching *The Parent Trap* and *The Sound of Mus*
What would it have been like to have parents who ador
her? As she'd grown older, her fantasies had turned
boys. She'd watched old Doris Day movies and dream
about a handsome man wanting to marry her. She'd fa
tasized about John Travolta falling for *her* instead of Oli
Newton-John in *Grease*. But her dreams had shriveled a
now lay dormant in her heart. Her prayers had never be
answered.

She certainly couldn't tell Cole. Her needs might jeopardize the family they'd formed.

"You never had anyone love you? Even your folks?" he asked.

She leveled her gaze on him. "I grew up in an orphanage."

"What?" He stared at her, his gaze intense, probing. "Oh, Elise." He paused, and she felt the uncomfortable weight of his pity. "So that's what you meant when you said your parents wouldn't have come to our wedding."

"They didn't show up for the first part of my life, why would they want to be there for the next phase?" She shook her head. "Don't feel sorry for me. I'm used to it. I always wanted a family, and you gave me one. For that I'm grateful."

She watched as his throat worked up and down, the muscles contracting and surging. "I don't pity you. Hell, I had a family, but it wasn't all I wanted it to be. In a way, we suffered the same loneliness. 'Deserted' is a scary place to be."

"You get used to it."

"Do you?"

She swallowed the sudden rush of tears. No one had ever pushed beyond her pat answers. No one had ever cared enough.

"Not really," she answered honestly, truthfully, facing it fully for the first time. But now it didn't seem so frightening. Maybe because she knew she had Cole and Haley. "You've been there yourself, haven't you?"

He shrugged. "It's one thing to have a love affair go sour. It's worse to have your child rejected. The pain is deeper, more intense. And you feel incredibly helpless, unable to ease your baby's suffering."

Understanding burned inside her heart. Rusty had rejected both her and her baby. But she'd been given a chance to fix the situation. A chance with Cole.

"You can understand how Haley feels."

"I know," she said quietly, her heart filling with a strange emotion she'd never experienced. She'd never met anyone who could empathize with her, never had someone who tried to connect with how she'd felt all those years. It brought a sense of peace to her soul that had never been there.

"It's not easy for me to trust again," Cole said, his gaze drifting off as he became more reflective. "Must not be easy for you, either."

She nodded. Could they ever bridge that distrust to find love again? "I'm scared. I waited for a long time to find a family. Then I'd thought I'd found a home—even a traveling home was better than none—with Rusty. But he dumped me. I'm scared this might be too good to be true. That I'm going to wake up from a dream, or realize it was a figment of my imagination. I'm scared to love again."

She looked away. When she spoke next, her voice was strained, her hands shook with powerful emotions. "But I want love more than anything. I thought I could live without love. But a family without love is like an empty shell, meaningless. Can we…could we ever trust each other enough to…"

She stopped herself, unable to say what she really wanted, to hope that her dreams could really, finally come true.

Cole weighed her words carefully before speaking. "I don't know." He ran his hands down his jeans. "I worry you're going to pack your bags and leave like Paula did. I know that sounds stupid. You've never done anything to make me think you'd walk out on us. But, even though I'm not a child like Haley, my fears are as real as hers

It's hard to trust again. I don't want…Haley's heart broken.''

''Or yours,'' she added, reading the pain saturating his eyes and feeling it deep inside herself, too.

He remained silent, not agreeing, but not denying, either. The truth resonated in her soul, shattered her heart.

''I don't want to love someone, anyone—even you. But honestly, Elise, you make it damn hard not to.''

Her heart stopped.

''You make me long for something that seems impossible.'' Cole's voice touched a raw nerve inside her. ''But I'm too damn cynical to believe in fairy tales.''

Staring into Cole's intense gaze, she felt optimistic. Hope rose out of the painful mist of the past. Maybe there was a solution. Just maybe something could be done to help both of them live happily ever after.

''Can you help me,'' he asked, his voice cracking, ''to believe again?''

Chapter Nine

How did one invite a man to bed? With a seductive off-the-shoulder negligee? With a subtle taking of his hand? With a bold question? Elise didn't have a clue. It was a stupid idea.

She knew better, knew the raw pain that making a mistake like this could cause. She also knew the potential end results. The only difference this time was that a marriage contract bound Cole and her together. Supposedly, til death do they part. But not necessarily with a happy ending. So, why was she doing this? Why couldn't she let their relationship remain the same?

Because she wanted, and needed, more than a polite marriage. And she sensed Cole wanted more, too. Hadn' he said as much? The only way to get what they both wanted—love—but were too afraid to hope for—was for her to take a risk to prove her trust in Cole.

The tension between them was her fault. She'd kept them apart, thus preventing them from making a true commitment with their bodies and souls. She was scared to let

Cole inside her heart. She was afraid he'd no longer want her to be a part of his family.

Now, it was up to her. She had to figure out a way to tell Cole of her plan. Should she be subtle? Bold? Coy? Brazen? She had to step over the line dividing them. She had to make the first move. Because of the agreement she'd forced Cole into, he never would. Since she was the one who'd put up the barrier, she had to be the one to knock it down. Even though the outcome might devastate her.

She reminded herself that Cole wasn't like Rusty. Her feelings for Cole went much deeper than anything she'd even imagined with her ex-boyfriend, but it made the risk that much greater. Her stomach was jittery with nervous energy as she waited for Cole to bundle the blanket and put the leftovers into the picnic basket. She remembered when she'd surprised him with that first visit and her proposition. He'd stood at the edge of the porch, his skin glistening with sweat. Once again, excitement spurted through her veins.

He stepped around her and opened the door, giving her heart a start. He gave her a warm smile that caused a lump to form in her throat.

Trying to draw a breath, she stared up at the night sky. Stars winked and blinked against the inky backdrop. Night sounds of crickets and bullfrogs indigenous to the west Texas countryside sounded as loud as a freight train roaring in her ears. Or maybe it was the rush of blood pulsing through her.

Cole set the basket inside the door and waited for her to enter. She took two steps into his family's ranch house and paused, uncertain and apprehensive. There was a legacy of love in this house, starting with Cole's great-great-grandparents. She wanted to bring it into their marriage.

But could she? Was she, a little orphan girl, capable of continuing that legacy?

Darkness closed in around her, intensifying her senses. She heard Cole's breathing behind her, smelled the musky scent of his cologne, felt his hand brush against her waist. Anticipation, mingled with doubt, shimmied down her spine and caused goose bumps to rise along her skin.

When he reached for the light switch, she stopped him with a hand on his arm. This would be easier in the dark.

"What is it?" he asked, his tone husky. He stood so close to her she could almost feel his hard body pressed against hers. In fact, she yearned for it.

"Don't…" she breathed, struggling to formulate her thoughts into speech. "D-don't say anything. Not now."

Words weren't necessary. She clasped his hand, making a tender, tentative bridge between them, and linked her fingers with his. Their palms pressed together, generating heat that spread throughout her body like a flame burning out of control.

Turning into the darkness, she tugged on his hand and pulled Cole along behind her. She made her way to the stairs with only slivers of moonbeams cutting through the window blinds to guide her. Her heartbeat doubled as they began the slow, customary climb to the second floor. But this time everything was different.

Tonight, Cole wouldn't be sleeping on the floor.

"Elise," he said, his voice steadier than her legs felt when they entered the bedroom. "What are you—"

"Shh." She turned toward him and placed her hands on his shoulders. "Don't say anything. Please."

She felt the heat of his body, the strength in his muscles, the tension making him stiff with uncertainty. She ached to feel his arms about her, longed for him to make the next move.

What should she do now?

A breathy silence fluttered between them like the erratic beat of her heart. *It's your decision, Elise. If you want this, if you want to risk everything on a slim chance for a happy ending, then you have to make it happen. Now.*

With the ticking of the clock on the bedside table loud in her ears, she felt like Cinderella about to hear the chime of midnight. Would all her hopes disappear like the pumpkin carriage if she didn't take this chance? Wishing she had a fairy godmother, or any mother, who could provide sound advice, she inched toward Cole, shuffling her feet with hesitation.

The toe of her boot bumped into his. Her hands tightened on his shoulders, squeezed the hard muscles. He grasped her waist, and a slow sizzle burned through her clothing to her skin.

It seemed as if they were both waiting, both teetering on the brink, both holding their breath. *It's up to you, Elise. Cole's a gentleman. He won't make the first move. Not when he promised he wouldn't.*

Sliding her hands along the hard edge of his shoulders, she heard the rasp of his shirt beneath her palms, felt the strong sinews along the back of his neck and the rough texture of his hair under her fingers. On tiptoe, she tilted her head and angled her mouth to fit against his.

"Do you know what you're doing?" His whisper grazed her lips and jolted her like a shock of electricity.

She froze. A halo of moonlight surrounded his tall frame, hiding his features in shadows. Sensing more than seeing his expectant stare, she wished the darkness could swallow her whole. Would he put a halt to her foolishness? Would he back out before she could?

What if he did? He'd already told her he wanted her. She had to trust him, even when every fiber in her trembled with fear. If he backed away from her now, she knew i would be because he feared loving again. The night shad ows gave her courage.

"I know exactly what I'm doing." Her voice no longe trembled. She sifted her fingers through his hair, grazin his scalp with her nails. She heard his rough intake o breath, felt his chest expand, his hands tighten around her waist. Smiling with a sudden surge of power she'd neve experienced before, she lowered her voice and asked, "Do you?"

He chuckled, making his chest rumble. "I thought I did Now I think I've forgotten everything...even how to kiss.'

"You remember."

"What are we doing? I thought you said you didn't wan this—didn't want an intimate relationship."

She needed to have his mouth on her, to forget the dis cussion, but he held her an inch from him, resisting, prob ing, making certain this was the right move. "I changed my mind."

"There's no going back after this," he warned.

"I'm only going forward. Are you coming with me?"

His hand cupped the side of her face with such tender ness that tears surfaced, blurring her vision. In a gruff bu tender voice, he said, "I don't want you hurt, Elise."

He was the only one who could hurt her, yet his word destroyed the last of her reservations. No one had ever pu her feelings first. No one had ever cared enough. Not he biological parents. Not any of the couples who'd inter viewed her for a potential adoption. And certainly not Rusty.

But Cole had. Which meant that in his own way he cared. Maybe more than she could imagine.

Her heart tumbled the rest of the way into love, building up momentum with each passing second. Tired of his questions, afraid of the answers they might find, she muttered, "Shut up."

Then she kissed him.

His arms came around her in that instant. Their mouths melded together and she allowed her body to dissolve into him. Her bones seemed to melt. She had to hang onto him so she wouldn't become a puddle on the floor.

A tremor rocked through her at the simple, yet complex, touch of lips against lips, flesh against flesh. She tilted her head and leaned into him, accommodating, shifting, blending. His hand slipped down to her neck, and his thumb rubbed along the ridges of her throat, making her pulse skitter.

She opened to him, needed him. Of their own accord, her hands tested that wide expanse of shoulders. His muscles were solid, his skin hot beneath his cotton shirt. She felt him tremble with suppressed desire.

She needed this—the reassurance. She'd been on her own for so long. She closed her mind to everything but the feel of Cole's mouth against hers. His clean, fresh taste aroused her. His warm, masculine scent made her feel safe and secure—if only for a moment. But it was enough for now. She clung to him with a desperation of someone hanging off the edge of a cliff.

His tongue swept through her mouth, brushing over hers, tasting, licking, delving deeper. The rough stubble on his cheek sensitized her to his every nuance. A warm glow started low in her belly and spread to her limbs.

She ached for more, and a sense of urgency drove her. She pulled him toward the bed where she'd slept night after night alone. His hands explored her body, moving over her with eager, daring urgency. Every nerve ending exploded with the bombardment of sensations.

Cole pressed her back until she lay on the mattress.

Moonlight slanted across the bed. She could no longer hide in the darkness.

"You're beautiful," he said, his voice thick.

With his bold stare sweeping over her with the impact of an intimate caress, the dark center of his eyes burning like coals, smoldering and hot, she felt loved.

"I don't want to hurt you," he repeated, "or the baby." His concern and consideration touched her.

"You won't." She took his hand and pulled it toward her as an invitation.

His fingers unbuttoned the front of her dress, his knuckles grazing a bared stretch of flesh. He spread his hand across her stomach, curling his fingers inward, as if he'd pull from her all she was, all she had to give. She gasped, and her stomach muscles flinched.

"Did I hurt you?" he asked, worry deepening the lines around his eyes and mouth. "The baby?"

She blinked, confused. "N-no. I'm okay. The baby's okay. Please, Cole, don't stop."

He shook his head as if with disbelief. Slowly, his hand uncurled and his fingers splayed across her abdomen and moved lower still. Tingles of pure sensation rippled through her, settling low and pooling in a warmth of desire.

A moan escaped her parted lips, and she reached for him, tugging at his shirt. She wanted to touch him, run her hands over his chest. She fumbled with the first few buttons, then slipped her hands inside. A mat of fine hair covered his chest, whorling around his nipples, and arousing her with rough, erotic sensations.

His hand eased inside the dress. Longing coiled inside her. Slowly, he filled his hand with her breast, brushing his thumb over her filmy lace bra. The roughened but gentle pads of his fingers aroused her to heights she'd never dreamed of. With each gentle kneading motion, each sweet torturous grazing of her nipple, waves of excitement rolled through her, making her insides undulate.

He settled himself over her, fitting his body against hers. His hard arousal pressed against her with an urgency she, too, felt. "Oh, Elise," he mumbled against her mouth, his breath ragged. "I need you."

Her heart lurched madly. She wrapped her arms around him and clutched him to her. If only this could last. If only he could love her the way she loved him.

As he peeled away the layers of her clothes, the last of her reservations and doubts disappeared, too. In Cole's arms, with the heat of their bodies fueling a fire inside her, she no longer felt alone. Her hand touched his chest.

His heart beat wildly. Never had he felt so complete, so connected to anyone. His body tightened with need, but he held back and took his time. When he shed the last of his clothes, he rested on his forearms above her, feeling her heat draw him to her.

"Are you sure this is safe, I mean, for the baby?"

She smiled and touched his face. "You better not be thinking of stopping now."

Slipping her hands to his lower back, she pulled him toward her, and he entered her. He watched her face for any sign of pain or discomfort.

A moan escaped her parted lips. "Please, Cole, now."

Dipping his head and nibbling the length of her throat, he found his rhythm. She moved with him, driving, urging him faster until he sucked in a breath, held it until his lungs burned. He gritted his teeth, moving, sweating, waiting for her.

Suddenly she arched her back, her body tensing. She cried his name softly into his ear. Then he found release inside her, hot and sweet. He buried his head against her neck and allowed the shudders to crash over him.

Legs entwined, they lay together on his bed—their bed now. It took a few moments for Cole's breathing to steady and his heartbeat to slow. He smoothed his hand along her back as she curled against him, her hand resting on his chest.

"Are you okay?" he asked.

She nodded, her hair brushing his shoulder, teasing him. "Perfect."

He chuckled softly and tucked her securely against his side. "And the baby?"

She took his hand and placed it over the delicate swell of her stomach. "Very content."

Beneath his palm he felt a tiny flutter, like a butterfly's wing. His heart contracted. His breath snagged on a lump of emotions he'd never expected.

Her light laughter lilted through the room. "Did you feel it?"

"Was that the baby?" he asked, his voice rough with emotion.

"Yes." She smiled at him, her fingers combing through his hair.

Slowly, reverently, he eased his hand over her abdomen, hoping to feel the tiny movement again. He imagined what it would have been like to feel Haley move at this stage. His chest burned with regret.

"How long have you been feeling it move?" He traced the contours of her stomach with his fingers, memorizing the feel of her, the softness of her skin, the gentle swell where the baby grew inside her. He'd never seen a more beautiful body. Being pregnant only made Elise more so.

"A week or so."

He felt a sharp jab in his gut. "But you didn't say anything."

She shrugged. "I guess I didn't think you were that interested."

Shame gnawed at him. "I'm sorry."

He wanted to share this pregnancy with her. If she'd let him. He'd been shut out by Paula and missed so much. Now he wanted to know what Elise was feeling and witness the changes in her body. He cupped her full breast, weighing it in the palm of his hand, awed by the power of nature, the beauty of Elise.

"I've been so damn selfish." Inching upward, he brushed his thumb along her jaw line. "I was trying not to go crazy by focusing on the changes in your body. So I tried to keep my distance. Since you weren't interested in..." He dipped his head, feeling awkward about discussing his feelings.

"In sex?"

"Yeah."

She sighed. "I didn't want just sex. I wanted something more. I wanted..." She drew her bottom lip between her teeth. "I thought I only wanted a family. Sex was what got me in trouble with Rusty. How I ended up like this. I thought it would jeopardize everything."

"But what about tonight?"

"I decided to take a chance on you." She brushed a finger over the dimple in his cheek.

"Even though you're pregnant?"

She laughed. "That doesn't mean I don't have desires." Her hand on his face stilled. "Didn't you and your ex-wife ever make love while she was pregnant with Haley?"

He flinched. Admitting what he'd never told anyone, he said quietly, "Never. Paula wouldn't let me near her. I thought every pregnant woman felt that way. It's one reason I've been keeping my distance from you. I thought that was why you made me agree to no sex. I thought it would pass.''

"It was fear. I thought if we made love that I'd lose you. The way I lost Rusty.''

He leveled his gaze on her. "Do you miss Rusty now?''

"No.''

A long silence followed. Elise's hand idly caressed the back of his neck. In an astonished voice she said, "You didn't ever feel Haley move inside your wife, did you?''

He shook his head.

"Oh, Cole.'' Wrapping her arms around him, she held him close.

He luxuriated in the feel of her silky skin against him, in the strength of her emotions, in the depth of her understanding of his pain. He never wanted this time together to end. For the first time ever he felt bound to someone—to Elise.

"I want to know more about you...about what you're experiencing with this baby.''

"You can ask me anything.''

"Do you regret being pregnant?'' he asked, his thoughts drifting toward her relationship with that cowboy she'd followed out west.

"No.'' She took a deep breath. "I just regret Rusty. I thought you and I would have a better chance of forming a family without making love. But I've learned that love is the basis for a family. It starts with the parents. And making love is simply a way to express that love.'' She lifted his face to meet her steady, solemn gaze. Her hazel eyes sparkled in the moonlight. "I love you, Cole Dalton. That's why I wanted us to make love tonight. And I hope...some day...you can love me, too.''

His pulse quickened. Tenderness swelled inside his

hest, choking him. Joy sang through his veins. He loved
er, too. Already she had given him so much more than
e'd ever imagined. His arms tightened around her, held
er to him. He couldn't get close enough, couldn't get
nough of her.

But fear froze the words in his throat.

He loved her. But he feared the power she held over
im, feared being destroyed by her. After Paula, he'd
owed never to love again. Still, the truth pounded through
im with every beat of his heart.

Knowing he had to answer her declaration, he covered
er mouth with his, kissing her thoroughly. Maybe dreams
lid come true after all.

Happy birthday to you...

A pale pink glow seeped into the room. Elise lay on her
ide, her heart pounding. Now she'd have to face the con-
equences of her actions. Once again.

Some birthday, huh?

She'd told him she loved him. *Stupid, Elise! Really stu-
id!* He'd answered her with silence.

He didn't love her. He'd *never* love her.

She felt the sharp stab of rejection deeper than ever be-
ore. When would she learn to keep her mouth closed?
When would she learn to lock up her heart and throw away
he key? Humiliation burned inside her. She rolled onto
er back and stretched, feeling her tired muscles groan
vith pleasure.

Once again she lay in the wide bed all alone. Cole had
isen before daybreak and tiptoed from the room carrying
is boots in one hand. She cringed at having to face him
gain. Maybe she could delay it as long as possible.

Flinging back the covers, she stood. Her image in the
val mirror caught her by surprise. She stared for a mo-

ment at her full breasts, the slight roundness of her tumm
Cole had lavished attention on every part of her, almo
reverently, treating her with such care and concern. S
blushed at the memory of his kisses and explorations. He
been curious about her pregnant body, eager to please he
tender yet strong.

He'd loved her. He had. She wanted to scream her fru
tration. But doubts haunted her. Maybe she'd been wron
so very wrong about him.

Turning away from the mirror, feeling too vulnerab'
too alone, she dressed quickly. She scribbled a note th
she'd gone to pick up Haley and left it on the breakf:
table.

"Now that looks like a woman in love," MaryAnn sai
as Elise walked through the door of her beauty shop.

Elise felt a prickly heat rise along her skin. Her he:
had been ripped from her chest.

"Yep, she's got that exhausted look," Beth Thomps·
nodded with a sly grin.

"It was their anniversary last night," MaryAnn e
plained to the curious onlookers. "How'd you like t'
fancy restaurant Cole took you to? He's turned into a b
spender now that he's in love."

In love? Right! Elise felt the barbs of those words.

"I brought your dress back," she said, wanting to avo
any personal discussion.

"Oh, great." MaryAnn's smile evaporated.

"And I thought I'd pick up Haley early."

Concern knitting a frown in her forehead, MaryA·
studied Elise closely. "Sure. I let her go play in the pa
with some other kids."

"Okay, I'll pick her up there," Elise said, needing sor
fresh air. "Thanks, MaryAnn."

"Any time, sugar."

Before Elise could push her way out into the sunlight, MaryAnn stopped her with, "Oh, I forgot! Somebody came by here looking for you."

Confused, Elise turned. "For me?"

MaryAnn nodded. "A man...a cowboy."

Bewildered, Elise frowned. "Did he say what he wanted?"

"Just you, I guess. His name was Rusty something."

Elise's heart stopped cold. "Uh...MaryAnn, could you watch Haley for a while longer?"

Chapter Ten

*I*diot! *What were you thinking?*

Cole cursed himself with each step. He lifted the saddle off the buckskin mare. Winnie whiffled and stamped her hoof impatiently.

"I'll be back and brush you down," he mumbled.

He stalked to the tack room, the room Elise had reorganized. Everywhere he looked he saw touches she had brought to the ranch, alterations she had made. But the most significant change was in Haley and himself. His daughter had the family she'd so craved. She seemed happier, more carefree. And somehow, miraculously, Elise had opened his heart to the possibility of love.

Then why didn't you tell her that, you jerk?

"I will." He surprised himself by speaking out loud. Rubbing the sweat off the back of his neck, he grabbed the tools he needed to groom his mare.

As soon as he finished his chores, he was going to bake a birthday cake for Elise. Then he was going to give her the birthday present he'd wrapped first thing this morning. *Then I'll tell her I love her.*

"What are you doing here?" Elise asked, fear shredding her insides.

Rusty Jones stood beneath the awning of the barbershop, his Stetson tipped back revealing his sun-bronzed face. Still tall and lanky as a willow branch, he wore his usual faded Wranglers and T-shirt. A grin, the one that had first attracted her to the cowboy, emerged. "Hey there, sugar! I've been looking all over the place for you."

He swooped her up in his arms and twirled her around, making her dizzy. When she landed on her feet, the funny feeling in the pit of her stomach disappeared. *He* didn't make her dizzy, not the way Cole did. The old feelings had vanished as quickly as the dust had settled when Rusty drove out of town without her.

She remembered the pain, but felt it now more acutely because of her unborn child. Rusty hadn't simply rejected her. He'd turned his back on their child. Anger set her jaw. "Why did you come back?"

"I've got a rodeo in Amarillo tonight and I wanted to see you again. I didn't know if you'd still be here or not. But I took a shot at finding you." He reached for her. "Come on, sugar, let's go get a bite to eat and we'll talk."

This time she sidestepped him. "You can say whatever it is right here."

Then Elise noticed the gazes staring from across the street at Chuck's Diner. Waitresses she once worked with peeked through the curtains. Church members she'd met over the last few weeks gawked. Neighbors and friends of Cole's speculated on what she was doing talking to this stranger. She knew all too well how tongues would wag with this tidbit of gossip.

She cringed as she relived Rusty's exuberant hug. Wha
would folks here think? She didn't want to humiliate Col
or embarrass Haley.

"Let's go somewhere private." She started walking to
ward Cole's spare pickup, the one she often used to tak
Haley to and from school.

"All right, sugar. Whatever you want." Rusty fell int
step with her. "I'm staying in the motel on the edge o
town. We can go there."

Cole downed another glass of lemonade and munche
on the cookies Elise had made. The lopsided chocolat
birthday cake sat in the middle of the table, the candle
ready to be lit. He felt the antique wedding ring, the on
his great-great-grandfather had given his mail-order brid
burning a hole in his pocket. He tapped his fingers on th
note Elise had left on the kitchen table. What was takin
her so long?

As the afternoon withered beneath the relentless heat o
the Texas sun, his impatience to uncork his bottled emo
tions exploded into worry. Had something happened? Ha
that darn pickup broken down on the highway?

Angry at himself for letting her drive the cantankerou
truck, he regretted not buying her a new car. He woul
though. As soon as possible. But first he had to find Elis
and Haley.

Reaching for the phone, he dialed Jack's number. Afte
it rang twelve times, he realized MaryAnn would be work
ing and had probably taken Haley to the shop with her
He disconnected the call and tried again.

"Cut and Curl."

He recognized Beth Thompson's twangy voice. "I
MaryAnn around?"

"Sure thing. It might take her a minute she's givin' somebody a rinse. Hang on."

Before he could explain this was an emergency, he heard a clatter over the line and knew the phone at the shop was dangling by the cord, swinging into the wall. He could hear the muffled sounds of a hair dryer, and then high pitched laughter, which set his nerves on edge. Gritting his teeth he waited.

"This is MaryAnn. What can I do for you?"

"Have you talked to Elise?" He dispensed with the formalities.

"Cole?"

"She left a note saying she was on her way to pick up Haley." He stared down at the toe of his boot hoping that Elise had just left with his daughter and was headed back to the ranch.

"Uh..." MaryAnn hesitated. "Haley's still here. Elise asked me to watch her a little longer."

"Did she go shopping?" he asked, relief starting to sift through him. At least he knew where his daughter was. "Elise was complaining that none of her clothes fit any more."

"I don't think so."

Concern gripped his gut. "Was she feeling okay?"

"As far as I know."

"Then where could she have gone?" he asked more to himself than MaryAnn. He shoved his fingers through his hair with frustration. "Did she say anything to you?"

Suddenly a cold clamp tightened around his spine. *No. Not again.* His gaze landed on the note she'd scribbled, obviously in a hurry. Had she left because he hadn't told her his feelings? Had she left for good? Without an explanation? Without even a goodbye? Like Paula?

"Um, Cole, I think she might have gone looking for..."

MaryAnn's voice dropped to a whisper. It sounded as i
she had cupped the phone with her hand. "This man came
looking for her earlier. When I told her...well, she wen
white as a sheet. That's when she asked me to watch Haley
for a while longer. Do you know who could've been look
ing for her?"

Cole's knees buckled, and he grabbed the counter fo
support. It had to be that cowboy, the one she'd loved, the
one who'd gotten her pregnant.

Damn. This time the fault was his. He hadn't given her
a reason to stay.

"Marry me, sugar." Rusty sat on the orange-and-green
comforter spread across the motel's double bed. "I've de
cided it's the right thing to do."

Elise had experienced some interesting proposals in her
time. Once again it wasn't the heart-stopping romantic
kind. It was plain, simple, on the same scale as if he'd
asked her to pass the salt. Irritation surged through her
"What?"

"Hell, I panicked. Wouldn't any man who learned he
was gonna be a daddy? But I've come to my senses.
wanna do the right thing by you and that baby."

"I can't." She sat in the desk chair that was missing
the slats along the back. "I can't marry you."

"Now, I know I was wrong. I apologized, didn't I?"
He leaned forward, bracing his hands on his knees.

She looked her ex-boyfriend in the eye, not feeling
smidgen of regret or an ounce of desire. "I'm married
Rusty."

His brown eyes widened. "You are?" He doffed his
Stetson and hooked it over his knee. The hatband had
creased his sandy blond hair. "Since when?"

"We've been married a month."

He rubbed his brow with his thumb. "Who is it?"

"A rancher who lives near Desert Springs. You don't know him. His name is Cole Dalton."

Rusty slapped his hand against his thigh. "You were just pullin' my leg then when you said you were pregnant."

She shook her head. She had to tell him the truth. "No. I really am pregnant. And the baby is mine. Not yours. You gave it up when you walked out the door. And I'm not yours anymore, either. I'm married now."

"Well, I'll be." Rusty stood and paced along the bottom edge of the bed. "Didn't take you long to find somebody to replace me."

"No," she admitted, realizing the truth of his words. She'd found someone better, someone she loved with all her heart. Even if Cole didn't love her. "It didn't."

He faced her then, his brown eyes narrowing. "Do you love him?"

"Yes," she whispered, pain tightening her throat. She dipped her chin, tried to hide the tears that pressed, hot and urgent, against the backs of her eyes.

Rusty started pacing again, scuffing his boots along the nubby sage carpet. "I guess you want to stay married to this fellow."

Her heart contracted. Pain resonated through her. "I don't know."

Not if Cole didn't love her. She couldn't bear the thought of his not returning her love. Seeing him every day would drive a spike into her heart. She wouldn't be able to withstand the pain. Unable to stop the sudden flow of tears, she tilted her head in her hands. Could she take away her baby's chance for a real family? Could she stay, loving Cole, and never receiving his love in return?

"Damn." Rusty stood beside her, his hands on his hips. "What did I say?"

Her shoulders shook with suppressed sobs.

"He treating you right?" Rusty asked, his voice suddenly gruff.

She cried harder. Cole had treated her fairly—he just didn't love her. He'd never love her.

"If he's laid a hand on you—"

She grabbed Rusty's arm. "N-no. I'm okay. He hasn't hurt me." Physically. "H-he doesn't l-love me."

Rusty's tense features relaxed. "How come you married him if he don't love you?"

She drew in a shaky breath. "Because I was scared." Pushing a cuticle back with her thumbnail, she clasped her hands tightly together. "Because I thought…I don't know anymore."

Frankly, she'd admitted too much to Cole. Pain resonated in her chest.

Rusty's face crumpled into worry lines. "That so?"

Sniffing, she nodded, unable to speak.

"Well, then, sugar, I say do what you want. You can either stay married to him. Or you can come along with me. I'm headin' to Vegas for a rodeo in the mornin'. We can get married there, if you want. Your choice."

She wondered if this was the best offer a girl like her could hope for.

Cole saw his truck parked at the Flame Motel. Anger spurred him into action. By God, he wasn't going to let Elise leave him this easily. He loved her. He just had to tell her. But first he had to stop her. Because he couldn't live without her.

"Charlie!" He shoved open the door to the manager's

office. "There's a stranger staying here. His name's Rusty. What room is he in?"

Through half-glasses, Charlie Hood glanced up from the paperback he was reading. "Hey, Cole. Haven't seen you around in a while. Things going well with that new bride of yours?"

"Yeah, okay." Cole tapped the counter. "About that stranger, could you check on that room number?"

"Oh, yeah." Charlie swiveled his chair around and studied the room assignments. "He's in fourteen."

"Thanks." Cole rushed out the door.

The sound of his boot heels echoed as he clomped along the sidewalk. Anger pumped through his veins. Each breath came hard and fast. His mind spun with possibilities. None of them palatable.

When he reached number fourteen, he refused to hesitate, knock or wait. His wife was in there. Alone. With another man! The man who'd made her pregnant!

He reared back and kicked the door in. The pain shooting from his heel right up his leg didn't register in his brain. He rushed into the room and took in the scene. The cowboy knelt in front of Elise as tears streamed down her face. Rage rocked through Cole. Had the son of a gun hurt her?

As the cowboy rose to his feet, Cole stepped forward, cocked his arm back and gave the stranger a good solid jab to the jaw. Reeling backward from the blow, the cowboy lifted his arms in self-defense.

"Whoa, there," the man said.

Cole moved forward again, ready to pummel the guy.

"Cole!" Elise cried, reaching out to stop him. She grabbed his arm and held onto his shirt. "Stop! What's gotten into you?"

"Me?" He turned on her, all the fear and pain rising to

the surface. "You're the one who's in a motel room with another man. A man who isn't your husband!"

Her hand gentled and smoothed the material over his chest. "Cole, it's not what you think."

Anger gave way to desperation. He clutched her shoulders. "Look, Elise, I was wrong. I was afraid. I know it's not a good excuse, but it's the only one I have. I don't know why I couldn't say it last night. But the simple truth is that..." He swallowed his fear and took the plunge. "I love you."

He took a steadying breath. He felt stronger for having spoken the words. "I love you," he said again for good measure. He almost laughed out loud at the sheer joy it brought him. But the solemn wariness in Elise's gaze sobered him. Had he spoken the words from his heart too late? "Did you hear me?"

She gave a slight nod, but her features remained frozen.

"I think I've loved you for a while now, but I couldn't admit it even to myself."

"Cole—"

He panicked, his blood turning to ice in his veins. "Don't leave me, Elise." When she winced, he realized he was squeezing her shoulders too hard. He loosened his grip but refused to let her go. "Give me another chance. I'll prove it to you. I promise."

"Oh, Cole—"

"I know I have a lot to learn about being a good husband. But I'm willing to learn. I need your help. I need you, Elise. Please..." His voice broke.

Tears sprang to her eyes, and she launched herself at Cole. His arms came around her automatically. Stunned, he held her close.

he felt like heaven on earth. When she looked up at him, love shining in her eyes, he kissed her.

An awkward cough pulled them apart. Cole glanced at Elise, and then at the cowboy. The man gave a sheepish grin and said, "Seems like a strange time for introductions. I'm Rusty Jones."

Cole hesitated, immediately wanting to dislike this man. He had recognized the name of the one who'd hurt Elise. But then, if Rusty hadn't walked out on her, she wouldn't have been desperate enough to marry Cole. Shaking his hand, he said, "Cole Dalton."

"You got yourself a good woman," Rusty said. "You're a lucky man. I was dumb enough to let her go. Don't you be."

"I won't." Cole pulled Elise close to his side, his arm around her shoulders.

"If you ever need anything, sugar, just let me know." Rusty kissed her on the cheek and headed for the door, hooking his duffle bag over his shoulder. Before he left, he turned one last time. "If you don't mind, let me know what the kid is...a boy or a girl, okay?"

Elise nodded and her arm slipped around Cole's waist.

When the door closed and they were alone, they faced each other. Cole's pulse thrummed. "What'd he come back for?"

"Me." Elise laughed. "Can you believe that?"

Cole kissed her. "Yes." Then he kissed her more thoroughly. "You're some kind of woman, Elise Dalton. I've been trying to tell you that, but I'm just going to have to do a better job."

"It's taken me a long time to learn I'm not unwanted, that I'm good enough. Old beliefs die hard."

"Well, you just keep listening to me, darlin'. You're the best, Elise. The best woman. The best wife. The best mother. I couldn't imagine anyone more perfect for me...for our family."

"You mean that, don't you?"

"Every word." He held her tight against his chest. "
have to admit I was jealous of Rusty when I saw him here
with you. I thought…"

She covered his lips with the tips of her fingers
"There's nothing for you to be jealous of. He asked me
to marry him. And I told him I loved my husband." She
nuzzled against his chest. "I think he was more relieved
than hurt. He was just trying to do the right thing."

Cole pressed his hand to the side of her face, caressing
the soft skin of her cheek, smoothing her hair behind her
ear. With all the tenderness that welled in his heart he
kissed her, teasing the corners of her mouth and claiming
her for himself.

"Do you want your birthday present now or later?" he
asked, his voice rough with emotion.

"B-birthday? How did you know?"

"You have a fairy godmother, didn't you know?"

"No, I didn't." Her arms tightened around his neck
"No one's ever given me a birthday present."

He held her close, feeling her body tremble against him
"Then we have a lot of lost birthdays to make up for."

He dug in his pocket for the present he'd wrapped early
that morning. Dropping to one knee, he took her hand in
his and placed the ring on Elise's finger that his great-
great-gandfather had given his own mail-order bride. With
love filling every fiber of his body, he said, "I love you
Elise. Marry me."

Her mouth curved into a gentle smile and she slid down
to her knees. She gazed at him with such love and devotion
that his chest tightened. Tenderly, she caressed his face
"I already did. Remember?"

"I remember everything about that day. But I want you
to marry me again, this time for real, this time when we

both mean it.'' His hands roamed down her backside, enjoying the contours of her shape. ''So, will you marry me again, darlin'?''

She pushed playfully against his chest. ''I'm pregnant.''

He chuckled. ''You were pregnant last time, too.''

''But I wasn't showing.''

He shrugged. ''So we'll wait till our one-year anniversary, and then we'll renew our vows. We'll reserve the church, hire a band for the reception and really do it right. And this time, we'll have a real honeymoon.''

''To Disney World?''

''Hell, no. We'll go somewhere where we can be alone. Without any distractions. I want to concentrate on loving you.''

She slipped her arms around his neck and pressed her body against his, stirring more than emotions inside him. She cut her eyes toward the bed. ''Do we have to wait a year for that honeymoon?''

Dipping his head to kiss her, he scooped her up in his arms. ''Let's go home.''

''What about Haley?''

''She's with MaryAnn. Let's concentrate on us for a little while longer.'' Carrying her out the door, he walked toward his truck. ''Come, my lady, your carriage awaits.''

Epilogue

"Momma, read story."

"What kind?" Elise asked, folding back the covers on the small bed.

"One with happy ever after."

Elise laughed. "They all have happy endings, sweetheart."

"I'll pick one," Haley volunteered bounding onto her little sister's bed. "I'll even read it to you, Mallory."

"You will?" the three year old, with her momma's hazel eyes, asked.

"Sure. I'm the best reader in my class. My teacher says so."

Elise smiled down at her two daughters. She bent and kissed them both. "If you'll read Mallory a story, Haley, then I can go talk to your daddy for a few minutes."

She left the girls and wandered down the hall. A secretive smile curved her mouth, and her heart raced with excitement. She'd been waiting all day to have a moment alone with Cole.

She found him in the bathroom, a fluffy white towel wrapped around his torso. His bronze skin glistened with water droplets. She reached around behind him and hugged him close.

"Hmm. What a way to end the day." He turned and wrapped his arms around her. His skin smelled fresh with soap and cologne. He kissed the top of her head. "Want to go to bed early?"

She smiled up at him and welcomed his kiss. "I want to tell you something first."

"About the baby?" he asked, his eyes sparkling, his grin widening.

Surprised, she leaned back. "You know?"

He chuckled and tightened his hold on her. "Then it's true?"

She nodded, joyful tears welling up in her throat. "How'd you know? I haven't been sick."

"You were glowing."

She slapped his backside gently. "Bull. I've been tired and you know it."

He nodded. "What if I told you a man can sense these things?"

"I'd laugh."

Grinning, he kissed her again. "I love you so much."

"And I love you." Her eyebrows slanted into a frown. "But how'd you know? I was going to surprise you."

"Believe me, I'm surprised." He grasped her hands, linking his fingers through hers. "And I've never been happier. This is what I always wanted. A house full of kids. And you."

Tears flooded her eyes, and her heart expanded with inexplicable happiness.

"You're not going to cry, are you?"

"Probably." She squeezed his hands and sniffed. "Let go tell the girls."

He nodded. "Let me get dressed."

"Promise me the news isn't all over town." She gave him a sly grin.

"Not yet." He slanted his gaze toward the trash can. "Not unless you bought that pregnancy test at the grocery store."

"Oh, no." She groaned.

Grinning, he said, "Well then, we'd better tell the girls."

They padded down the hallway toward Mallory's room. The door was partially open and they paused before entering.

Elise motioned for Cole to wait beside her. "Aren't they sweet?"

Cole smoothed his hand down Elise's hair and rested his hand at her nape. Tingles rippled down her spine. Reaching up she covered his hand with her own.

Haley turned the page in the book. "Then the groom kissed the bride."

"Another one of their fairy tales?" Cole whispered.

Elise shook her head. Memories poured into her head as she stared at the white satin-covered book. "No, it's our wedding album."

"What next?" Mallory asked, looking up at Haley, her strawberry blond curls bouncing.

"First they had a baby. Then they got pregnant again," Haley said, her chubby hand tracing the figures in the pictures.

Elise met Cole's gaze. "She knows."

He nodded.

"Then," Haley said with the supreme authority only an eight year old could muster, "they lived happily ever after."

* * * * *

Soldiers of Fortune...prisoners of love.

Back by popular demand, international bestselling author **Diana Palmer**'s *daring and dynamic* Soldiers of Fortune *return!*

Don't miss these unforgettable romantic classics in our wonderful 3-in-1 keepsake collection. Available in April 2000.*

And look for a **brand-new** *Soldiers of Fortune* tale in May. Silhouette Romance presents the next book in this riveting series:

MERCENARY'S WOMAN

(SR #1444)

She was in danger and he fought to protect her. But sweet-natured Sally Johnson dreamed of spending forever in Ebenezer Scott's powerful embrace. Would she walk down the aisle as this tender mercenary's bride?

Then in January 2001, look for THE WINTER SOLDIER in Silhouette Desire!

Available at your favorite retail outlet.
*Also available on audio from Brilliance.

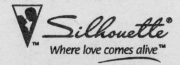

Silhouette®
TM
Where love comes alive™

SILHOUETTE'S 20ᵀᴴ ANNIVERSARY CONTEST
OFFICIAL RULES
NO PURCHASE NECESSARY TO ENTER

1. To enter, follow directions published in the offer to which you are responding. Contest begins 1/1/00 and ends on 8/24/00 (the "Promotion Period"). Method of entry may vary. Mailed entries must be postmarked by 8/24/00, and received by 8/31/00.

2. During the Promotion Period, the Contest may be presented via the Internet. Entry via the Internet may be restricted to residents of certain geographic areas that are disclosed on the Web site. To enter via the Internet, if you are a resident of a geographic area in which Internet entry is permissible, follow the directions displayed on-line, including typing your essay of 100 words or fewer telling us "Where In The World Your Love Will Come Alive." On-line entries must be received by 11:59 p.m. Eastern Standard time on 8/24/00. Limit one e-mail entry per person, household and e-mail address per day, per presentation. If you are a resident of a geographic area in which entry via the Internet is permissible, you may, in lieu of submitting an entry on-line, enter by mail, by hand-printing your name, address, telephone number and contest number/name on an 8"x 11" plain piece of paper and telling us in 100 words or fewer "Where In The World Your Love Will Come Alive," and mailing via first-class mail to: Silhouette 20ᵗʰ Anniversary Contest, (in the U.S.) P.O. Box 9069, Buffalo, NY 14269-9069; (In Canada) P.O. Box 637, Fort Erie, Ontario, Canada L2A 5X3. Limit one 8"x 11" mailed entry per person, household and e-mail address per day. On-line and/or 8"x 11" mailed entries received from persons residing in geographic areas in which Internet entry is not permissible will be disqualified. No liability is assumed for lost, late, incomplete, inaccurate, nondelivered or misdirected mail, or misdirected e-mail, for technical, hardware or software failures of any kind, lost or unavailable network connection, or failed, incomplete, garbled or delayed computer transmission or any human error which may occur in the receipt or processing of the entries in the contest.

3. Essays will be judged by a panel of members of the Silhouette editorial and marketing staff based on the following criteria:

    Sincerity (believability, credibility)—50%
    Originality (freshness, creativity)—30%
    Aptness (appropriateness to contest ideas)—20%

    Purchase or acceptance of a product offer does not improve your chances of winning. In the event of a tie, duplicate prizes will be awarded.

4. All entries become the property of Harlequin Enterprises Ltd., and will not be returned. Winner will be determined no later than 10/31/00 and will be notified by mail. Grand Prize winner will be required to sign and return Affidavit of Eligibility within 15 days of receipt of notification. Noncompliance within the time period may result in disqualification and an alternative winner may be selected. All municipal, provincial, federal, state and local laws and regulations apply. Contest open only to residents of the U.S. and Canada who are 18 years of age or older, and is void wherever prohibited by law. Internet entry is restricted solely to residents of those geographical areas in which Internet entry is permissible. Employees of Torstar Corp., their affiliates, agents and members of their immediate families are not eligible. Taxes on the prizes are the sole responsibility of winners. Entry and acceptance of any prize offered constitutes permission to use winner's name, photograph or other likeness for the purposes of advertising, trade and promotion on behalf of Torstar Corp. without further compensation to the winner, unless prohibited by law. Torstar Corp and D.L. Blair, Inc., their parents, affiliates and subsidiaries, are not responsible for errors in printing or electronic presentation of contest or entries. In the event of printing or other errors which may result in unintended prize values or duplication of prizes, all affected contest materials or entries shall be null and void. If for any reason the Internet portion of the contest is not capable of running as planned, including infection by computer virus, bugs, tampering, unauthorized intervention, fraud, technical failures, or any other causes beyond the control of Torstar Corp. which corrupt or affect the administration, secrecy, fairness, integrity or proper conduct of the contest, Torstar Corp. reserves the right, at its sole discretion, to disqualify any individual who tampers with the entry process and to cancel, terminate, modify or suspend the contest or the Internet portion thereof. In the event of a dispute regarding an on-line entry, the entry will be deemed submitted by the authorized holder of the e-mail account submitted at the time of entry. Authorized account holder is defined as the natural person who is assigned to an e-mail address by an Internet access provider, on-line service provider or other organization that is responsible for arranging e-mail address for the domain associated with the submitted e-mail address.

5. Prizes: Grand Prize—a $10,000 vacation to anywhere in the world. Travelers (at least one must be 18 years of age or older) or parent or guardian if one traveler is a minor, must sign and return a Release of Liability prior to departure. Travel must be completed by December 31, 2001, and is subject to space and accommodations availability. Two hundred (200) Second Prizes—a two-book limited edition autographed collector set from one of the Silhouette Anniversary authors: Nora Roberts, Diana Palmer, Linda Howard or Annette Broadrick (value $10.00 each set). All prizes are valued in U.S. dollars.

6. For a list of winners (available after 10/31/00), send a self-addressed, stamped envelope to: Harlequin Silhouette 20ᵗʰ Anniversary Winners, P.O. Box 4200, Blair, NE 68009-4200.

Contest sponsored by Torstar Corp., P.O. Box 9042, Buffalo, NY 14269-9042.

PS20RULES

ENTER FOR A CHANCE TO WIN*

Silhouette's 20th Anniversary Contest

Tell Us Where in the World You Would Like *Your* Love To Come Alive... And We'll Send the Lucky Winner There!

Silhouette wants to take you wherever your happy ending can come true.

Here's how to enter: Tell us, in 100 words or less, where you want to go to make your love come alive!

In addition to the grand prize, there will be 200 runner-up prizes, collector's-edition book sets autographed by one of the Silhouette anniversary authors: **Nora Roberts, Diana Palmer, Linda Howard** or **Annette Broadrick.**

DON'T MISS YOUR CHANCE TO WIN! ENTER NOW! No Purchase Necessary

Where love comes alive™

Name: _____

Address: _____

City: _____ State/Province: _____

Zip/Postal Code: _____

Mail to Harlequin Books: **In the U.S.:** P.O. Box 9069, Buffalo, NY 14269-9069; **In Canada:** P.O. Box 637, Fort Erie, Ontario, L4A 5X3

*No purchase necessary—for contest details send a self-addressed stamped envelope to: Silhouette's 20th Anniversary Contest, P.O. Box 9069, Buffalo, NY, 14269-9069 (include contest name on self-addressed envelope). Residents of Washington and Vermont may omit postage. Open to Cdn. (excluding Quebec) and U.S. residents who are 18 or over. Void where prohibited. Contest ends August 31, 2000.

PS20CON_R